The Divorced Kids Club

The
Divorced
Kids
Club

AND
OTHER STORIES BY

W.D. Valgardson

A GROUNDWOOD BOOK
DOUGLAS & McINTYRE
TORONTO•VANCOUVER•BUFFALO

Groundwood Books/Douglas & McIntyre
585 Bloor Street West, Toronto, Ontario M6G 1K5

Distributed in the USA by Publishers Group West
1700 Fourth Street, Berkeley, CA 94710

We acknowledge the financial support of the Canada Council for the
Arts, the Ontario Arts Council and the Government of Canada through
the Book Publishing Industry Development Program for our
publishing activities.

Canadä

Canadian Cataloguing in Publication Data
Valgardson, W.D.
The divorced kids club and other stories
"A Groundwood book".
ISBN 0-88899-369-2 (bound) ISBN 0-88899-370-6 (pbk.)
I. Title.
PS8593.A53D58 1999   jC813'.54   C99-931254-5
PZ7.V34Di 1999

Design by Michael Solomon
Cover illustration by Fiona Smythe/Reactor
Printed and bound in Canada by Webcom

To Jordan

Contents

The Entertainer and the Entrepreneur

The problem with summers, Tracy thought, was that there wasn't any school. Not that she wanted classes and homework or anything like that. It was just that once school was over, the kids all disappeared. She missed her friends.

The perfect summer would be one where everyone went to school as usual but there were no classes. There'd just be clubs and sports and projects. The teachers would be there to help you do whatever you wanted to spend your time doing and to keep some of the roughnecks in line. Tracy hated the Disrupters who slouched through the halls and wore their caps backwards. Their pants dragged on the ground and their faces scrunched up in disapproval whenever anyone tried to actually accomplish something. She'd once told her mother that and then heard her mother tell her father that if they weren't careful, they were going to have a daughter who was an old maid by the time she was fifteen. Tracy hadn't talked to them for two days.

The biggest Disrupter of them all was Shawn Benn. He was the kind who wore his cap to bed. His pants were so baggy, two other people could have got in with him and still had room to move.

"Boys would pay more attention to you," Tracy's mother said, "if you relaxed a little. Even businesses have casual Fridays."

There was no point talking to her mother. Her mother's idea of how things worked was from the sixties. Sometimes she even wore granny dresses and bangles. She looked like an artifact in the museum. Tracy had tried to explain to her that in the nineties there was no point being hippy-dippy, that life was tough and going to get tougher. If you were going to have a nice apartment and leather furniture and little red car, you had to give yourself an edge. You couldn't spend your time singing folk songs and worrying about whether the person who picked the grapes for Safeway got a fair wage or not.

Her father understood her better. He had to earn a living. First he'd started a shop that sold beads and tie-dyed clothes. Then he'd had a herbal shop and, finally, a health food store. He still had the health food store. It sold basmati rice, fresh apple juice, organic vegetables and ten thousand and one vitamins, stuff like that. Still, it was a business, and he'd had to get in touch with reality.

"Money," Tracy said, "means choices. No money, no choices. I want lots of choices. Like do I go to Paris for a vacation, or visit India? I've got plans and to make them work I need good grades and I need a job and I need bucks in the bank."

"Babies do get switched at birth," her mother said, standing in the kitchen, her arms full of flowers. The inside of their house was like a flower shop. Tracy had tried to get her mom to set up a stand at the front of the yard and sell bunches of flowers, but her mother had just shaken her head in dismay. She put them out with a sign saying FLOWERS FROM THE UNIVERSE. FREE. HAVE A GOOD DAY.

"You're a nerd," Shawn Benn said to her one day.

"When I turn eighteen, I'm going to start putting a thousand bucks a year into an RRSP," Tracy retorted. "When I'm sixty-five, I'll be a millionaire and you'll be a street person."

"I'm going to have my own band," Shawn snapped back.

"I'll throw a buck into your guitar case when I go by," she said.

"I'll bet I make twice as much money as you this summer," he said, twirling his cap around and around his finger. He balanced it on its brim, then flipped it into the air.

"Over my dead body," Tracy exploded.

Tracy told Betty, her best friend, that she was going to get a job.

"You're too young," Betty replied. "Who's going to hire you?"

"Fake it until you can make it," Tracy said.

She put on some make-up, tailored pants and a jacket, borrowed ID from one of the older girls and visited the stores in the mall. They all told her to come back in a couple of years.

"Ageism," she shouted when she got home. "I'm going to go to Human Rights and charge them with ageism."

"Why don't you go to the beach instead?" her mother replied. "Cool off with a swim."

Tracy took her beach towel and sun blocker and a book on the stock market. She was trying to figure out the way to go. Becoming a broker was one possibility. She had a list of the richest people in Canada. There were no musicians on the list, nobody with a band. There were CEO's of companies like Magna International or stock promoters. Another possibility was to become a lawyer and then a politician and then go into business for big bucks. She lay on her beach towel thinking about riding around in a Mercedes-Benz.

She was nearly asleep when she felt sand spray over her back. She opened her eyes and looked up. Shawn Benn was standing there with his guitar case.

"You said you were getting a job," he said.

"I've decided not to work for anyone else," she answered. "I'm an entrepreneur."

"You're unemployed." He headed down the beach. He stopped at a bench along the beach sidewalk, took out his guitar and started to play. It was a good spot. A lot of tourists went by there on the way to the dock. Tracy could tell that some of them were throwing money into the case because she saw it glint as it fell.

She ran down to the water and jumped in. She dove under the water, then surfaced and swam as far as the line of floats that marked the swimming area. As she was treading water, she looked back at the long curve of beach. It was packed with people from the city. On weekends, the glare of suntan lotion was blinding.

She swam back to shore.

"Unemployed," she hissed under her breath. How dare Draggy Pants call her unemployed. "I am Woman," she said to herself. "I can do anything." When she said that it usually helped her get through things like being teased about her hippie parents. It had helped her survive having a mother who was a poet. It helped her survive the other kids seeing poems her mother had written about her. They kept appearing in the local newspaper. On the days they appeared, Tracy skipped school.

Today, it didn't help to take the sting out of Shawn's words. She'd told everybody that she was going to get a job. Step one in her climb to the top. She even had pictures she'd cut from magazines of women who were executives.

None of them went around with beads and bangles. She couldn't imagine Margaret Witte or Margaret Thatcher with flowers tucked behind their ears wandering around the house in their bare feet. She was even considering changing her name to Margaret.

She wished she'd brought a cold drink with her. There were only a few trees and already there were families with kids and picnic baskets under them. She was only six blocks from home but it seemed like miles. She really didn't want to walk all the way there for a drink and then all the way back. The restaurant was at least half a mile down the beach.

Reluctantly, she got up and walked to the restaurant. There was a group of six or so people standing listening to Shawn. As she walked past, he stopped whatever he was singing, then started to strum the guitar as he sang, "Be kind to the unemployed, don't make fun of them, they'll be destroyed." She strode right by but she couldn't help noticing all the coins and a few bills lying in the guitar case.

To get her drink she had to stand in line. Sipping on it, she wandered along the dock. Her dad's old boat was there. It was sort of a punt, square at both ends. She often rowed around the harbor in it. There was really only room for one person but sometimes Betty came with her.

Standing there, looking back at Shawn, at the beach, at the people, taking a sip of her drink, Tracy had an idea.

"An entrepreneur," she'd said, but she'd really not been thinking of being an entrepreneur. She'd been thinking of getting a job, working for somebody else.

"Sure," her father said, when she asked permission to use the boat. He said sure to most things. Otherwise, he said "Peace," and made a V with his fingers. He even said sure when she asked if she could have the half can of purple paint in the basement. She scrounged six thin aluminum poles from behind one of the garages, then ransacked the attic until she found one of her mother's old striped ponchos.

She took the poles to the school. She knew Mr. Marks, the shop teacher, worked in the classroom even during the holidays. She showed him what she wanted and asked him if he would help. He drilled holes into the aluminum and found some wing nuts to attach to them. Tracy wasn't sure how to attach the cloth, but she kept repeating to herself, "Where there's a will, there's a way."

She painted the punt purple, stuck the aluminum poles into the gunwales and put a screw through each one to hold it in place. Then she attached the extra aluminum rods to each pole to make a rectangle.

"I need help," she said to Betty. "This is a buddy job."

The poncho was brightly striped—red, green, yellow. Any time her mother wore it, you could see her from six blocks away. Tracy had wished her mother wore clothes that didn't look like a walking neon sign. Now she was glad about the bright colors.

Betty helped her fit the poncho over the aluminum frame. The center part where her mother's head usually stuck through was a problem, but Tracy shrugged and said, "I'm not going to be doing this in the rain. Besides, the idea is just to get people's attention."

She brought the family's foam cooler filled with ice and soft drinks down to the beach on a wagon. She and Betty wrestled it into the boat.

"Be careful," Tracy said. "It's tippy with the canopy on it."

She'd put on a yellow T-shirt and red pants and a large sun hat. Then she and Betty got into the boat and Tracy rowed around the sailboats and fish boats and out of the harbor and down the outside of the dock toward the shore. It was a Saturday and there were a lot of people lying on the beach, even though it wasn't yet noon.

Tracy had tied a sign to the top of the poles: COLD DRINKS FOR SALE—$1.50. She'd paid fifty cents for each drink, so she only had to sell twenty of them to do better than babysitting all day.

"Oh, look," Betty said. "There's Shawn." Whenever he was around, she always started to flutter and giggle.

"He's too busy being an artiste to notice us," Tracy said. "He's lost in Bach's Concerto Number Nine."

"No, he's not," Betty said. "He's playing 'Yellow Submarine.' I have to go now. I've got to babysit my little brother."

Tracy nosed the boat into the beach. She noticed that for all of Betty's uncommon hurry to babysit her brother, she had time to stop and listen to Shawn.

Tracy was going to be Betty's friend until she died and maybe after that, but at times it was a trial.

She began to row slowly along the shore. At first no one seemed to notice, but then a man in a red bathing suit and a sunburn yelled, "Hey, you. Bring me a drink."

Tracy grabbed a can of pop, jumped into the water and took him the drink. He gave her a dollar fifty.

She sold six drinks on her first tour of the beach, then seven on her way back. She made three more trips and sold thirty drinks altogether.

When she got back into the harbor, her arms and back ached. She felt her nose. In spite of the canopy and sunblocker, it felt tender. Her eyes hurt and she knew that she was going to have to wear sunglasses to protect them from the glare from the water.

Shawn was still on his bench when she went by. As she approached, he started to sing "The Good Ship Lollipop." Tracy threw a quarter into his guitar case. "An entrepreneur," she said. "Not unemployed."

The next morning when she woke up, she thought she was going to die. She tried to move one arm, then the other, but moving hurt so much, she decided against it.

"Chamomile tea," her mother said. Her mother's cure for everything was chamomile tea. Headaches, sprains, broken hearts. Tracy ached so much she was willing to try anything. "Windy out," her mother mentioned, peering out the window at her herb garden.

Tracy was grateful it was too windy to take the punt out. She wasn't able to lift her arms over her head until after one o'clock. The next day, though, she was back at the dock.

She loaded up the cooler. There weren't as many people because it was a weekday, but there were vacationing families. There weren't a lot of sales. One here and one there. Her dad had said that about the store. Good days and slow days. What was important were the averages. You had to be philosophical about the slow days.

Shawn, she noticed, was having a slow day, too. Hardly anyone was walking along the pathway, and those who did walked right by. It was the weekend tourists who were big spenders, who wanted to be entertained. The cottage people and the locals weren't interested.

"You're going to have muscles," Betty said. Betty was into flouncy dresses and berets and accessories. She wasn't sure that having muscles was the thing to do. She didn't want to be an executive. She wanted to marry one. She taped the soaps. One entire wall of her basement had tapes of soap operas. Tracy couldn't figure out why they were friends. Betty was so frivolous. If she had to work, she'd said once when they were having a sleepover, it would be in some place where she'd meet someone rich and let him fall in love with her. Her mom and dad both had two jobs, a day job and a weekend job each.

The next day when Shawn took up his place on the bench, he had a mouth organ on a metal frame that he wore over his shoulders. That way he could play the mouth organ and the guitar at the same time.

"He's an idiot," Tracy said to Betty. The extra music seemed to get people to stop more often, though.

"Maybe," Betty replied. "Maybe he's just desperate. I've heard he can't get a penny from his folks. Anything he's got he pays for."

The weather had turned cool, and fewer and fewer people were coming to the beach. The parking lots were mostly empty. Some days there were long stretches of empty sand.

"Diversify," her father said when she showed him the three or four dollars that she was taking in for a day's hard work. "Add more product."

The next day Tracy added dry ice and another cooler and filled the cooler with Popsicles and Freezies. She rowed up and down the beach, waving to the few people lying on the sand. She put on her friendliest smile. She ran up the beach delivering drinks without muttering under her breath about people too lazy to come down to the boat. As she went by sunbathers, she said, "Cold drinks, Popsicles, Freezies, potato chips."

She got so she could row all day without getting sore. At night she fell asleep and slept like a log until her alarm went off in the morning. She was able to sleep in because hardly anyone came down to the beach before ten. Then she'd get up and organize her goods and pull them down to the dock.

Shawn was mostly playing to himself. The large crowds strolling the boardwalk had faded away. People were staying locked up in their houses in the city, watching TV. On the weekend, he tied a pair of cymbals to the insides of his legs so he could play the guitar, the mouth organ and the cymbals all at the same time.

"A one-man band," Tracy said contemptuously. "That's what he thinks he is. Next thing, he'll have a nose flute and be beating a drum with his foot."

"Isn't it great," her mother said, "that he can play so many different instruments." She was one of those people who, if you had a leg cut off, would have thought up all the wonderful things you could do with one leg. If you lost a hundred dollars, she'd think of all the trouble you could avoid by not having the money. It drove Tracy crazy.

"Get real," she'd mutter. "Bad's bad, good's good, awful's awful. Don't mix them up."

The music, she could see, wasn't paying any better than the pop and potato chips. Then Shawn didn't turn up for three days and she had the beach and all the potential customers to herself. The weather warmed up a bit and more people started bringing their blankets and beach umbrellas.

Every so often Tracy would stop rowing, throw her arms upwards and shout, "Hot, hot, hot," to encourage the sun.

On the fourth day after Shawn disappeared, he returned. Only he didn't have his guitar. Instead he brought a set of white and black dumbbells, which he juggled. As he flipped the dumbbells back and forth, he talked to the passersby. Sometimes he juggled brightly colored balls. Little groups actually gathered.

"Have you seen him?" Betty asked breathlessly. "He's really good."

"He should wear a clown outfit," Tracy replied. She was feeling miffed. She'd tried carrying Revellos but they'd gone soft and she couldn't sell them.

"I've got to take that out of my profits," she complained.

"Happens all the time," her dad said. "What do you think happens to my vegetables that wilt and the apples that get brown spots?"

"You bring them home and make us eat them," Tracy said.

As she rowed back and forth, she kept an

eye on Shawn to see how many people were stopping to watch him. She could see the colored balls flying through the air. When she got to the dock, he was sitting with his legs over the edge, looking down, pretending not to look at her, counting his money.

"I'll have a Coke," he said, throwing down two loonies. "Keep the change."

She was so angry she could have spit, but she handed him up his drink. A customer was a customer.

"I don't know why you hate Shawn so much," Betty said. "What'd he ever do to you?"

"I don't hate him," Tracy said. "What makes you think I hate him? You've got to think somebody's important before you can hate him."

"Right," Betty said.

"He's just so smug. He's always got to be the best. He's got to win."

"You don't like winning?"

"I don't go around showing off. I don't have to be the center of attention."

Tracy wondered if she might increase business if she had an amplifier and could announce that she had cold drinks for sale, but her dad said that wouldn't be allowed. Someone was sure to complain. After all, a lot of people went to the beach to lie in the sun and sleep.

"I've got to increase sales," she said. She kept seeing that roll of bills Shawn had been counting. It wasn't that she cared if he was making more than her but she didn't like making less than him. It wasn't even the money, really. It was just the idea. The idea that Baggy Pants was worth more than she was.

"You shouldn't judge people by how much money they make," her mother said. Her mother was hanging flowers upside down to dry them. They were her winter sunshine bouquets.

"Life is a game and the one with the most toys when he dies, wins," Tracy replied. She'd read that in a magazine. Someone worth one thousand gazillion bucks had said it. The opinion of people with one thousand gazillion bucks was worth more than the opinion of people who hung flowers upside down to decorate their houses during the winter. If you had gazillions, you could just order fresh flowers flown in on the Concorde.

Cold lemonade. Homemade. That, she thought, was the solution.

She bought the lemons, squeezed them, made the lemonade, froze the ice cubes, and figured that the profit margin on lemonade was greater than on drinks. She added a pitcher of lemonade to one of the coolers.

"I need a bigger wagon," she said to her father, but he just shrugged. "Don't overload the punt," he said. "You'll tip it."

"You should wear a life jacket," her mother said.

"Mom, be serious. I never go out past my waist. Nobody is going to buy drinks if they have swim out to me. Besides, I'm an excellent swimmer."

"Your mom's right about the life jacket," Betty said when they were alone.

"The only time I'm in deep water is when I have to go around the dock to the beach. It takes five minutes."

The days turned from hot to hotter. Too hot for people to stand in the sun and watch someone juggle. Instead, they headed straight for the water. When they lay on the sand, they set up umbrellas so they'd have some shade. Some days, Tracy sold all her stock and had to make a second trip to replenish it.

Shawn had taken to wearing a wide-brimmed straw hat. He moved to the shade of one of the scrubby maple trees, but he performed for himself and three or four little kids.

At first Tracy felt triumphant, but as the hot days stayed and no one went near the maple tree, she wasn't so sure how she felt. She walked by after a really good day and was going to put a loonie in Shawn's hat, but when he saw her approaching, he picked up his hat and put it on.

The next day and the next, he wasn't there.

"He couldn't cut it," Tracy said to Betty. It was a phrase her father sometimes used to describe people who were going to grow organic fruit or vegetables or bring herbs but who stopped delivering after finding out how much work was involved.

"Haven't you heard?" Betty said.

"Heard what?"

"He's working on a new act."

Two days later Shawn was back. He had a brightly colored umbrella on a long pole. As Tracy watched, he began to juggle with the balls, then added something that shone and glinted in the light. As she looked closer, she realized that he was juggling a knife along with the balls. People immediately stopped to watch.

"Ambulance chasers," Tracy said with disgust. "They don't care how well he juggles. They just want to see blood."

"You sound like you care," Tracy's mother said.

"He could get a haircut," Tracy said to her mother. "He could wear his cap forwards like everyone else."

"He'll grow out of it. In his India period your father went around in robes and shaved his head."

"You've got to dress like where you want to go, not where you are. Image matters."

"Maybe he wants to be someone different from you."

"Bo Bo the Clown," Tracy retorted. She wasn't forgetting his crack about her being unemployed instead of an entrepreneur.

The weather turned against her. It didn't storm but there were sudden gusts of wind that blew sand into people's eyes. The water was a bit choppy. It was just enough to keep people from swimming.

The weather didn't stop Shawn's juggling act. He kept adding objects. Coins glinted and spun toward his upturned hat. Most afternoons Tracy had to cart home nearly as many drinks as she had brought in the morning.

The second Saturday in August, when she got to the harbor, the water was choppy, the wind gustier than usual.

"You're not going out in this," Betty said.

"It's just around the dock and back into shore. He's ahead. I just know he's ahead."

She fitted the drinks into the punt, tightened the screws that held up the awning, settled onto the seat and rowed around the gas boats and sailboats. The day started well because a woman on one of the sailboats called her over and bought six drinks. Inside the harbor there wasn't a ripple on the water, but when she passed the mouth and turned to go to the outside of the dock, the water jerked and snapped all around her. The punt started to bob and weave.

She dug in the oars. She rounded the end of the dock, then rowed along the side. The outside wall was straight concrete. The chop kept banging the punt against the dock.

Tracy forced the little boat away from the dock. She was about halfway to shore when the punt started to rock from side to side. The awning made it top-heavy. She stood up to take the awning down and with that a sudden gust of wind toppled the boat.

Just before she went over, she looked up. People were lined up along the dock looking down at her. Shawn was watching as well. As she tipped, all she thought about was that she was going to look like an idiot and she was going to lose her drinks. She wasn't worried about having to swim. She was a good swimmer. But then the boat caught her and the awning tangled around her. She could feel the boat rolling over, pushing her under the water.

"Help!" she yelled.

There was a splash beside her. Someone had cannonballed into the water. The next moment, Shawn was thrashing around beside her. He grabbed the uprights and pulled them loose. With that, Tracy was able to pull free. She dog-paddled beside him. He was clinging to the overturned boat.

"Let's swim to shore," she said.

"I can't," Shawn said. He looked scared. "I forgot. I can't swim."

"You can't swim? Are you an idiot, or what?" A wave splashed in her face. "Let go of the boat and tip your head back. I'll tow you to shore. It's not far."

"I can't," Shawn said. "I'm scared of the water."

"Let go," Tracy replied. "I won't let you drown. I've taken lifesaving lessons."

She put one arm under his chin and began to pull. He let go. They didn't have to go far before they could stand on the bottom.

The waves were pushing the punt in behind them. The cooler was bobbing in the water.

"You can't swim and you jumped in to help me," Tracy said.

"I just forgot, that's all. You yelled help and I jumped. Then I remembered."

Everyone on the dock was watching them.

"If you'll help me drag the boat onto shore, I'll buy you fries and a dog," Tracy said. "I'll even throw in a Coke if you get hold of the cooler."

"You're an entrepreneur," Shawn said, dragging the cooler behind him. "You'll be a CEO some day."

"I'll come to watch you perform," Tracy replied. "I'll want the best tickets in the house. Okay?"

"Yeah," Shawn said. "That'd be great. The entertainer and the entrepreneur. That's us."

Cyberworld

"You're going to get into trouble," Carol said. "You're doing stuff you're not supposed to."

"I'm a hacker, not a cracker," Sam replied. "Don't bother me. I'm setting up a web page."

"Dad says you're spending too much time on the computer."

"He's a drooler," Sam sighed, turning away from his work. With Carol bugging him, he couldn't concentrate on writing HTML.

"He bought the computer."

"He plays games on it. He writes letters. That's like using Challenger to go to the store for groceries."

"You're a geek."

"I'm not a geek. I haven't got a clipboard. I don't use a pen protector."

"Since you started this computer stuff, you don't play ball, you don't ride your bike, you won't go swimming with me. Like, cyberspace isn't everything, you know."

"It's the future." Sam fidgeted with the mouse, moving the cursor around the screen. "There are kids writing programs. It doesn't matter how old you are. All that matters is what you can do. One kid I read about is making eighty thousand a year."

"There's more important things than..." Carol stopped. She couldn't finish the sentence. Money was very important to her. She was always going on about how she didn't get paid enough for babysitting. She was saving up for two weeks at a soccer camp.

"Bill Gates is a geek," Sam said. "He's the richest guy in the world. So there's geeks and then there are geeks."

"The kids are making fun of you."

"What kids?"

"Norman, Harold, Jackie."

"They think winning Minesweeper is the height of accomplishment."

"They're cool."

"Cro-Magnon," Sam answered. He knew that would bug Carol. She had a thing for Norman. He was always swimming or lifting weights or running. His heart's desire was to compete in the Iron Man competition.

Sam got off his chair and crouched down like an ape. He started shuffling across the room, grunting. He scratched his armpit.

Carol threw a pillow at him and left in a huff. Sam went back to his HTML. He was determined to get his web page up and running. He was going to put in some graphics. He was going to be a Webmaster.

"Where," he'd heard his mother once ask his father, "do you think he comes from?"

"I dunno," his father said. "A throwback, maybe. Uncle Boris could multiply or add faster than a calculator. He was on TV sometimes showing how he could do it."

Life was difficult, Sam thought. Sort of like everyone else was color blind while he could see color but couldn't explain it. He knew that his mother and father were teasing when they made jokes about babies accidentally being exchanged at the hospital. He wondered, though, why he was so different from everyone else in the family. He wished that Uncle Boris were still alive. Maybe it was from him that he'd inherited the ability to do algorithms. He knew that most kids didn't think math was fun. He tried to explain to them about how exciting numbers and formulas could be but gave up when he saw their eyes glaze over.

His mother clung to her electric typewriter with fierce devotion. It had a white erase ribbon that let her correct errors without having to use White-out.

His dad made a real effort. That's what was so distressing. If his dad had been one of those guys who didn't care or just didn't notice, it would have been different. But his father read books on how to be pals with your kids. It worked fine with Sam's older brother and sister, Greg and Carol. The three of them shot baskets and set up a net in the driveway to play one-on-one hockey. Dad shuttled them to hockey games, soccer games, baseball games. They took Sam with them, but he could never figure out why it mattered if someone threw a ball or kicked a ball or shot a puck farther than someone else. He tried. When everyone else jumped up and cheered, he jumped up and cheered, too, but his heart wasn't in it. Once he snuck a magazine article on the latest viruses out of his jacket. He was so busy reading it, he forgot to jump up when Greg's team scored the winning goal.

He remembered the story of the ugly duckling. It eventually turned into a beautiful swan and it wasn't an ugly duckling at all. It had just been put in a nest with ducks. He had been put in a nest with a bunch of Luddites.

Just as Sam was figuring out where he would rent advertising space, his father appeared in the doorway.

"Let's communicate," his dad said.

"Okay," Sam replied. "What about?"

"Whatever," his dad said. "Anything you'd like to communicate about. You know, a real father-and-son talk."

Sam wasn't sure what to say. His father was a professor in the faculty of education. His specialty was teaching people to be physical education teachers. He knew all sorts of things about team sports and track and field. He was good at golf.

"Do you think the Bombers are going to win the Grey Cup?" Sam finally said. His father could talk about the Blue Bombers for hours on end.

"Well, they've got a good offense but..." He

caught himself. "You don't want to talk about that sort of stuff. Let's talk about your stuff. Let's talk about RAM."

"RAM?" Sam said.

"Sure, or HTML. Any of those things. What're you working on now?"

"Clickable images."

Sam showed him the map tags. His dad's eyes were glazing over when Carol appeared and asked if someone would spot her on the trampoline.

When his dad went outside, Sam gave a sigh of relief, but he still felt terribly lonely. Being different was hard but he didn't see what he could do about it. It was like he was born speaking Chinese while his family spoke English.

"I think," his mother said at supper, "we need to put a limit on the amount of time Solitario spends on the computer."

Sam groaned quietly. When his mother used his full name, things were serious.

"If it's money you're worried about, there are other ISPs that give more time on line for the same fees," Sam protested.

"ISP?" his mother asked.

"Internet Service Provider," his dad said.

Sam was proud of his dad. He might need droolproof software, but he was coming along. He'd never be a cybernaut or anything, but with a little coaching, he'd be able to use a search engine.

"Speak English," his mother said. She had that look. There was no describing it. She just morphed into something tight. When he was five, he realized that she could morph. One moment she was giving him a cookie and the next she'd noticed he'd walked across the kitchen in his muddy shoes. It was like Jekyll and Hyde as he watched.

"The people we pay so that we can get on the Internet," Sam explained. He tried to put the cost in a positive light. "That way there are no long distance charges. You know, like when I sent that E-mail so you could order those special flowers. It would save us money if you sent E-mail instead of writing to Gran or talking on the phone." He didn't bother to mention that Gran had not been keen about his suggestion that she buy a computer. She had been even less keen about his suggestion that she take a course on how to use a computer. Dragging the family into the twenty-first century was proving to be a chore.

"No more surfing this month, Sam," his dad said. He put the ISP bill on the table. It was for fifty hours. The extra hours were at a dollar and a half an hour. He was speaking in that tone of voice that meant your mother and I have talked about this and made a decision. "You used up your time and everyone else's. You've got to learn to share."

"Carol uses it to play Pac Man," Sam said. "I'm actually doing something."

"You've got a computer at school," his dad answered. "You can spend some time on that."

"It's a 286."

"A computer is a computer," his mother said. "You don't have to have the latest of everything."

◆

The next day Sam stood in Miss Stevens' classroom and stared at the 286. Nobody used it except for playing computer games.

"A 286," Sam complained to his best friend, Arthur. "Why doesn't my mother go back to cooking over an open fire. Big chunks of dead animals on a spit. Washing clothes in the creek."

"Maybe it can be upgraded?" Miss Stevens said.

"It'd be great for anchoring a boat," Sam replied.

As Sam left the room, he bumped into Cro-Magnon Man. Carol was lurking behind him.

"I hear you got a flat tire on the cyber highway," Norman said.

"Pull a tendon," Sam replied and dodged out of the way.

The next morning was Saturday. Sam went over to Arthur's. When he got there, Mr. and Mrs. Smithers were packing their tent and supplies into their station wagon. The whole family was dedicated to creative anachronisms. They regularly joined a hundred or so people who dressed up in medieval clothes and pretended to be ladies and knights. Today, in honor of some saint's feast day, there was going to be a tournament.

Since his computer was unplugged, Sam agreed to join them. His parents thought it was such a great idea that they immediately signed a medical certificate giving Arthur's parents the right to allow a doctor to treat Sam if he got hurt.

He thought they might go somewhere exotic. Instead they parked at the top of a hill beside the water reservoir. Brightly colored tents were set up among the Garry oaks. Some people were putting up banners. A herald with a trumpet went by.

Sam helped set up the tent. That's when they informed him that he'd have to discover who he had been in medieval times.

"I'm thirteen," he said. "I wasn't even around in the seventies."

Mr. and Mrs. Smithers entered the tent in blue jeans and sweatshirts and came out dressed as Friar Prester and Lady Edith. Then Arthur disappeared, only to reappear as Morgun the Poacher. He had a couple of stuffed quail and a stuffed rabbit tied to his belt.

"Come with us," Mr. Smithers said to Sam. "We'll take you to the Channeler."

They led him to a woman sitting at a table. She had a set of Tarot cards before her.

"This young man," Mrs. Smithers said, "wishes to journey into the past to discover the person he once was."

All around them knights and ladies were

coming out of tents. There were page boys and minstrels. From the look of the people around him, nobody had been a dirt-poor farmer in those days, but at least half a dozen people had been King Arthur, including a woman. The Channeler explained that gender wasn't a characteristic that was passed on. It had something to do with developing the whole personality over the eons.

"A sorcerer's apprentice," Sam said in a panic. He wasn't keen on discovering that he might have been Lady Godiva. "I see moons and stars. I see crystal spheres." After they left the tent, people loaned him bits and pieces of costumes plus an abacus. At least, he thought, I've got a calculator.

They spent all day theeing and thouing while knights bashed each other and trumpets blared. He and Arthur weren't old enough to participate in the battles. They weren't even allowed to be water boys. In the evening they had an outdoor feast. No open fires were allowed, so they used gas barbecues.

And my folks think I'm strange, Sam thought as they ate supper while someone played a lute and sang ballads. They were mopping up stew with bread and a knife. There were no forks in medieval times, Morgun the Poacher explained.

"Now, wasn't it good to get out and be among real people instead of spending all your time in a virtual world?" his mother said when he got home the next morning. Little did she know that he was now called Urgul and his specialty was making poisons to rid the kingdom of pretenders to the throne.

That afternoon he and Arthur rode their bikes to a cybercafe and bought themselves soft drinks. They sat there watching the customers surfing the Net.

"I'm getting withdrawal symptoms," Sam said. "I've got to surf." He looked in his pocket. "I've got enough for fifteen minutes. That's just enough time to get on, get my E-mail and get off."

He could, he realized, practice his HTML without being on screen. He could build his page on paper. It was a strange idea. Using a pen to write seemed just about as strange as using a quill had the day before.

"You're far gone, Sam," Arthur said. "Time to check out the tourists."

They rode down to the harbor. The tourists were out in force. They were streaming into the Empress Hotel. They were being herded into red double-decker buses for a ride to Butchart Gardens. The Japanese honeymooners were holding hands and looking goopy. The Germans were strolling along in short pants and odd-looking hats.

"Stereotypes," Sam said. "They're all trying to be stereotypes. No one wants to be an individual anymore."

They rode around Beacon Hill Park. The daffodils were out. Large signs said PLEASE DON'T FEED THE DUCKS. All around the pools people were tossing stale white bread to the mallards.

"I wonder," Sam shouted to Arthur as they rode by, "if any of them has a laptop I could use?"

There were hang gliders over the cliffs. They were floating on the thermals. Big red and yellow and blue birds hanging in the sky, then swooping silently away only to swing back, catch a thermal and rise into the sky.

"You could sneak some time when your folks aren't home," Arthur suggested.

"Not a chance," Sam replied. "They've pulled the plug. How come you don't have a Pentium? What kind of a friend are you?"

"Normal. Let's check out the beach."

Sam could see why Arthur was Morgun the Poacher. That was his dark side. Normally, he was always pointing out birds and rabbits and seals. His plan was to become a game warden. He saw himself slipping silently through the forest, protecting Roosevelt elk and cougars and bears from the likes of Morgun. It had something to do with balancing good with his evil past.

They skidded down the cliff. The beach was covered in drift logs. Although they were huge, the logs had been thrown high up on the beach by the last storm. They lay side by side and over one another. Sam and Arthur walked along the logs, jumping from one to the other.

"Hey, Artie," someone called.

They stopped and looked around. There was no one in sight.

"Jane?" Sam shouted. He knew that voice. It had a sharp twang. Jane Smythe's family went to Texas for the holidays every Christmas, and she now talked like she'd herded cattle all her life.

Jane crawled out from under a shelter made of logs. Her blonde hair was done in cornrows.

"What are you doing here?" Arthur asked.

"Hanging out," she said. "Me and some friends. We're sort of living down here. Want to see my house?"

Drift logs had been propped together so they made a sort of rough tepee over a shallow hole dug in the sand. They had to get down on their knees to crawl inside. They couldn't stand so they sat facing each other with their knees pulled up.

"You've run away from home?" Sam said, incredulous. A lot of street people drifted to Victoria and lived on the beach, but Jane's family lived in a neighborhood where everyone had a gardener. When they were little, the three of them had gone to each other's birthday parties. One year her mother hired two clowns. Another year she arranged for them to visit a farm and ride ponies. They all got cowboy hats.

"Nah. Not so you'd notice. We just hang around here days and go home at night. No sleeping on the beach. The cops confiscate your pack sack and sleeping bag."

"Like camping out," Arthur said. He loved camping out.

"No plug-ins," Sam said. He crawled outside.

"What's with him?" Jane asked.

"Withdrawal symptoms," Arthur explained. He made like he was typing.

They crawled outside. Sam was sitting on a log, throwing stones into the ocean.

"Get a nose ring," Jane said. "Get your ear pierced. Get attached. There's people out there who have to beg to get money to eat."

"Your father drives a Mercedes," Sam said. He didn't want to be cruel but it was true. "Down here you're living in virtual reality."

"Gotta go," Arthur said. "He gets mean when he can't get his fix."

When Sam got home, his father was watching football on TV. The receiver fumbled the ball. "Lousy play, Sam. Did you see that? I could do better than that."

Sam studied his father. Sometimes Sam and his friends sat around and played let's swap dads, but when it came right down to it, he wouldn't have made the trade. That didn't mean he didn't have eyes. His dad was out of shape. He kept talking about starting to exercise but the weights stayed in the basement. His dad was addicted to Cheesies and potato chips and was always opening a bag when his mom wasn't around. He stuffed the empty bags into the bottom of the garbage can. Sam had caught him at it. He'd never played pro ball but he had been on the college team and he had made semi-pro.

His dad glanced at him but then the crowd roared, and his head snapped back to the screen. "Have you had a good time doing real things this weekend?" he asked over the sound of the TV.

"Max," Sam replied. "Absolutely max."

There was a world out there, Sam thought, and he could access it with the stroke of a key. Finland, Japan, Australia. He could talk to the world. He could call up pictures of distant cities, maps of neighborhoods in Helsinki or London. He could research mutual funds for his father and gardening for his mother. He could show his sibs more sports than they had ever dreamed of. There were virtual worlds in cyberspace that were crammed with all sorts of information for the real world.

As he stood in the doorway, watching his father imagining himself catching the ball better, tackling harder than the professional players, he thought about Arthur who dreamed of the day he could wear armor and participate in medieval battles, of Jane playing street person.

"Reality?" he said. "It's all cyberspace."

The Sand Sifter

"I don't care," Gisli said.

He didn't say what he didn't care about. I assumed he meant he didn't care in a general sort of way. When Gisli was doing a lot of thinking, he'd often say something that had nothing to do with what we were doing but with something in his head.

One time when we were sitting in Beacon Hill Park, he said, "Scary!" I didn't know him so well then. I swiveled my head around, figuring there had to be prep school kids in their uniforms or some bride and groom done up in a white dress and tux having their picture taken among the roses. There was nothing. Then I noticed his eyes weren't focused on anything. He was wandering around in the crevices of his brain.

School was going to be out in two weeks.

We were supposed to be in class doing a review for the math test that was coming up. Instead we were sitting on the beach catching some rays, our backs resting against the drift logs. The logs had been there so long we knew the worm holes and knots by heart. We had this favorite spot about halfway down the beach. It was a space between two big logs. We could sit with our backs to the sidewalk and look at the ocean and the boats and the people splashing by on the edge of the water. Or we could turn around and rest our backs against log number two and face the sidewalk.

When we did that, we said we were on chick patrol. But the truth is, there were no chicks. Just some moms with kids in strollers. The occasional jogger beating the cement with her feet. Mostly, though, the walkers were doggy people who wore identical jackets and carried little plastic bags to pick up dog poop.

The weather was unsettled. It would be still, then wind would kick up some sand and we'd be digging it out of our eyes. The wind was coming off the water so we had to make a choice: watch the wrinkle parade or get grit in our eyes. After a sharp gust, we shifted position. There were a couple of gray hairs following a gray poodle with a pink bow around its neck.

Maybe that's what made Gisli say, "I wish I had grandparents."

"Yeah?" I said. I was leaning back, my heels resting on a log. I wasn't thinking about grandparents. I was wishing I had seven bucks so I could go to the Sea Galley for a Neptune and fries. A Neptune's got a slab of fresh halibut. The fries are thick and home cut, not like the processed kind you get from the Food Fair. They come wrapped in newspaper and before you take them out, you douse them in malt vinegar and more salt than you should eat in a year.

I was in a burger frame of mind, and when I'm in a burger frame, stuff doesn't always get through to me right away.

"Yeah," he said. "You know, the kind who've got a farm somewhere and you can go ride horses or something. Maybe drive the tractor."

"You ever been on a farm?" I asked.

"Driven past some. That year we drove to the prairies. Those old wooden farmhouses and beat-up trucks have got to have grandparents living there. You know, the kind who're waiting at the gate when you get off the bus with your duffel bag. You can smell apple pie over the bus fumes."

"I guess," I said, searching in all my pockets. Sometimes miracles happened and I found a loonie or a toonie. If we'd been downtown, I'd have put my hat out and played something on the harmonica. I'm not very good on the harmonica, but you need to give people the feeling that it isn't straight charity. Everybody's got to have his piece of dignity, otherwise life's not worth living.

"You got any bills?" I said.

Gisli dug in his pockets. He came up with eighty-nine cents. I had thirty-four. It was nearly enough for a small fries. If all we got was a small fries to split, I'd end up chewing on the newspaper for the salt and vinegar.

"Life sucks," Gisli said. A rat came out of a hole under the sidewalk. Gisli picked up a rock and threw it at him.

"Hey, what are you doing?" I said. "That's Bernardo." I knew it was Bernardo because he had a piece of one ear missing. When we had fries we always saved a few for him.

"I don't care," Gisli replied. He threw another rock that glanced off one of the logs. Bernardo ducked back under the sidewalk.

That's how you miss out on being there for someone, even your best friend. You're thinking of burgers and fries and he's trying to tell you something. All he'd talked about for months was how he was going with his sister to stay with his dad in Calgary for six weeks in the summer. His dad had a house and a girlfriend there. He was a rigger in the oilfields and he was working close enough that he got to come home most nights. Gisli had been hoping that maybe there'd be something for him to do. Not like a real job. He wasn't old enough for a driver's license or anything, but maybe helping out on the side—cleaning tools and stuff.

Instead of listening, I was watching this guy in a lime green jacket and a Blue Jays cap scouring the beach for treasure. He had a metal detector for finding coins or rings or watches that people left behind. As he shuffled forward, he made little arcs with the detector. Every so often his headphones must have beeped, because he'd kneel down and use his sand sifter.

Most of the time all he found was pull tabs off soft drink cans.

I'd talked to him pretty regularly. At first it was hi, hi, but after that he'd stop to ask how I was doing. I got him to let me try the detector. If he was having a good day, he sometimes would spot me a loonie.

I went over to see what he'd found. "You got a new detector," I said. "Tesoro Lobo Super Traq." I read the name off the handle. He was concentrating on the sifting. He grunted, then stood up. He reached into the sifter and took out a quarter.

"That's what gets me out of bed in the morning," he said, laughing as he put the quarter into the pouch on his belt. "You don't have something to look forward to and life goes to hell in a hand basket." He'd been a logger until a tree had kicked back. He'd been banged up so bad he couldn't work anymore.

Sometimes he found rings. He figured when women were in swimming, their fingers shrank from the cold water. He'd found more than a few watches. Once he even found some false teeth.

"What's the matter with your friend?" he

said, looking over at Gisli. "Something biting his tail?"

Some kids had dug a pit and built a shelter with driftwood. Gisli was pulling it apart and heaving the logs as far as he could.

"I don't know," I said. "He has moods."

Just then a shiny blue van pulled up. It was one of those expensive ones that are supposed to be for rough back country but really get used to go to the grocery store. The driver got out and opened the back door. The Sand Sifter gave me a nudge. We both knew what was going to happen next.

Sure enough this newbie hauls out a brand-new chainsaw.

There are hundreds of logs. Big ones, small ones. They've been on the beach so long that they're no good for anything anymore. They've got so much sand in them that no one in his right mind would try to cut them up for firewood. Newbies don't know they shouldn't be burning driftwood because the salt will eat out the pipes in their wood stoves in a couple of years.

"I'd go and tell him but it wouldn't do any good, if you know what I mean," the Sand

Sifter said. "He's got this new five-hundred-dollar chainsaw and he's just desperate to try it out. I tell him he's going to wreck it and he shouldn't be burning driftwood anyway and he'll just get resentful. There's hard ways of doing things and easy ways. He prefers the hard way."

The Sand Sifter knew all about chainsaws. He was pretty interesting to listen to, talking about the trees he'd cut down and the places he'd been. It was hard to believe he'd run up and down trees, knocking the tops off. He still had a big chest from all that sawing and chopping, but now he dragged one leg when he walked.

One day when he'd made some good finds, he offered to buy me a burger but I said no thanks because I had twenty the old lady had given me for staying in school all week. He respected me for that. Not for making every class but because I wasn't taking something just because it was offered.

My old lady was real happy that week. "See, you can do it if you want to," she said, as if this was a surprise.

Gisli winged a rock off one of the metal lamp posts. "I'll see you later," I said to the

Sand Sifter. Gisli was still sitting in the same place. He'd used up most of the rocks within arm's reach.

"We could walk down to the harbor," I said to him. "We might pick up a few bucks from the tourists."

"To hell with it," he said. "To hell with everything." He got up and walked away.

I should have gone after him, I guess, but you know how it is. We've all got our own problems. My old lady and old man weren't having a honeymoon. She sat at the dining-room table and he ate his supper in front of the TV. After I was in bed, I'd hear them snarling at each other. Some mornings there'd be a blanket on the living-room couch and I knew he'd spent the night there.

When I went home, I was hoping that the school hadn't called about the missed classes. The old lady was into tragic looks and the old man was into yelling. If I told them Gisli had said he needed to go to the beach, they wouldn't have been impressed.

I was going to ask my mom to make burgers and fries, but it was too late. She'd already cooked stew and mashed potatoes and gravy. It was good. She's always reading cookbooks and watching cooking shows on TV. It just wasn't burgers and fries, and you know what it's like when you've got it in your head that you want something.

Maybe if there'd been burgers and fries, things would have worked out different. I'd have stayed home and watched TV and downed a bowl or two of popcorn.

Instead, Gisli called and we met at the corner. I was still thinking about those burgers and fries and I'd managed to get a ten-buck advance from my mom for promising to cut the grass the next day. The Galley was closed so we stopped at a corner store to get a package of cigarettes.

While I was explaining to the Chinese guy at the cash register that they were for my mom, Gisli suddenly started stuffing his sweater with chocolate bars and bags of candy and anything he could get his hands on. The crazy thing was that he wasn't trying to hide it. He was just standing there jamming all this stuff under his sweater.

The guy jumped over the counter as Gisli headed for the door. He grabbed Gisli's sweater and Gisli turned around and said, "What're you doing?" but all the stuff started falling out of his sweater. It was like this avalanche. The Chinese guy was trying to drag Gisli back into the store. He was pounding on Gisli's head and Gisli was swinging his arms and not landing any punches.

I came running up behind and gave the guy a shove. They both fell down and I tripped over them. We were all rolling around on the ground among the Oh Henrys and the jujubes, then Gisli and I scrambled up and started running. The guy was running after us, yelling his head off. Gisli was running so hard one of his shoes flew off.

We made it to Mount Tolmie. We were going up the rocks like mountain goats. There was a Mars bar stuck in Gisli's sweater. We sat down in the bushes. I stood up and threw the bar down at the guy. He was standing there yelling and waving his fist. We went down the other side and made a run for the bush at the university and got away.

It didn't do us much good. There was a cop car outside my folks' place when I got home. I sat behind the garage until it was gone, but I knew we were done.

The store owner brought Gisli's shoe to the station. Gisli wanted it back but the cops said they had to keep it as evidence. He confessed so he could get the shoe back. I said okay, I was guilty, too. What was the point in dragging it out? My folks weren't going to spend a thousand bucks on a lawyer. We figured it was a laugh because it was just shoplifting, but the prosecutor said Gisli had fought back and I had pushed the clerk so that made it assault for both of us. I was outraged. Kids pushed me around at school all the time. Nobody called that assault.

Before I saw the judge, my folks made me wash out the gel, get a haircut, lose the pin. They were mad. When we saw each other at diversion, Gisli looked like he'd just come from a private school. He was even wearing a tie. We didn't say anything to each other and my folks didn't talk to his mom. We both got two months' community service.

A couple of days later they gave me to this short guy who looked like he needed a shave. He had a bad haircut and he was just about as wide as he was tall. I'd never seen hands like his. They were big and the fingers were all flattened.

"You belong to me," he said. We were standing at the corner of this property with a bunch of old buildings and trees. There was this stone wall that went all the way around the property. I was dressed up like I was looking for a job in an office. He had on a pair of stained jeans and a red checked shirt with the sleeves folded up to elbows. "You go get dressed for real work. Get rid of sissy stuff."

I was choking on the tie but I still didn't like my clothes being called sissy stuff. The way he was looking at me, it was obvious that he wasn't just talking about the clothes.

My dad was sitting in the car. He had that grim, pissed-off look. If they still allowed it, he'd probably have had me publicly flogged.

I went home and put on old jeans and a shirt and the old man's workboots. I needed to wear two pairs of socks to make them fit, so my feet sweated like a pig. But I was going to be moving rock, and becoming a cripple at an early age didn't appeal to me.

"You see wall," George said. Except he wasn't George to me. I had to call him Mr. Papadopolous.

When I didn't say anything because it was

obvious there was a wall in front of us, he said, "You see wall?" This time I knew he wanted an answer.

"Sure," I replied. I even pointed at it just so we knew we were both talking about the same wall.

"Good," Mr. P. said. "Wall's falling down." That, too, was obvious, so I didn't say anything. "Wall's falling down," he repeated.

"Yeah," I agreed. "It's falling down."

He nodded. This, I realized, was not going to be a good summer. If I didn't do the community service, then it was juvie. I could tell my folks' aggro was at the limit. The old man had a short fuse at the best of times. He worked in sales and there was lots of pressure. He said he had nightmares in which no one needed refrigerators anymore. My old lady was easier. A day or two of cold looks and tight lips and then she was good for a hug and some apple pie. I wouldn't want to try and make her choose between us, though.

Mr. P. figured I was a moron. He kept showing me things I could see with my own eyes. You couldn't have a conversation with him. I tried to ask him some questions about himself.

That usually worked with the teachers. You asked them how long they'd been teaching or got them to explain some detail about whatever their favorite thing was, then they figured you were okay. It didn't matter so much if your homework wasn't done or you were fifteen minutes late for class.

Mr. P. didn't even bother to reply. It was like I was only there when he wanted me to repeat the obvious.

We walked the wall. Not part of the wall. The entire wall. It was close to a square block. Some of it went around the buildings but some of it went way back where there were blackberry brambles and lots of garbage. In places the wall looked good—well, not good, but it was still standing. In some places it had partly fallen down. In other places there were just piles of rocks.

Mr. P. bent down and picked up a chunk of gray concrete. He broke it apart with his hands.

"Mortar," he said.

I was learning the rules. "Mortar," I repeated, nodding.

He threw down the pieces of mortar. "No good," he said. "Not made good. Like some people."

Blame my mother and father, I wanted to say. I didn't have any part in it.

After our tour of the Great Wall of Victoria, he sat down with his thermos and poured himself a coffee. I figured since we were going to be working together and since nobody'd told me I was supposed to bring something to drink, he'd offer me some.

Not a chance. I took out a cigarette.

"You smoke," he said.

"Yeah."

"Not here," he replied. "Not good. Makes for cancer."

We drove to a building supply place, the kind your regular mom and pop can't go to. There were fifty-six guys who all looked like Mr. P. They were loading their trucks with sacks of cement and paving stones and stuff I'd never seen before. We backed up to a pile of bags of cement.

"You load," he said. Just to make sure I understood these highly intricate directions, he pantomimed the process. "You start here. You put there."

Some of his buddies were watching. I was sure they were wondering where he'd found this retardo who needed to be shown how to pick up and put down a sack of cement.

I started humping cement. It wasn't easy. The bags were heavy and hard to get hold of. They should have come with handles. I figured he'd be back in a minute to give me a hand. Instead, the truck was nearly full before he appeared with a couple of sheets of paper in his hands. He looked at me, then at his watch, put the papers in his shirt pocket and started lifting bags.

I knew that I wasn't supposed to be moving bags of cement. It was against the child labor laws, but I didn't think the old man was going to want to hear it.

I scrounged a bucket and thermos out of the basement for the next day. I loaded it up with peanut butter and jelly sandwiches, a banana, an orange and an apple plus as many brownies as I could fit in.

We started rebuilding the wall. I figured we were going to use a cement mixer but Mr. P. said the work was too slow for that much mortar. I mixed it in a wheelbarrow and he reassembled the stones. In lots of places stones had dropped out and were lying on the ground. These were easy to figure out. The places that made no sense were where a whole piece of wall had been knocked down by the frost.

After a couple of days, Mr. P. gave me a trowel. He showed me how to fill up the cracks. When he didn't like how I'd done it, he dug the mortar out and I had to do it again. I figured he was just being perverse because nobody was going to see the wall where we were working. Even if they did, nobody was going to take a close look and tell all their friends that there was a joint that wasn't quite right.

Mr. P. worked fast. He slapped down the mortar, piled the stones, made a good, thick cap to keep the water out. That, he said, was what was wrong when the wall was first built. The cap was no good and the water got in and it froze. Maybe it didn't do much damage the first year, but eventually it forced the wall apart. He was going to make sure this time that there was a good, strong cap.

I kept smashing my fingers. The first few times I hollered and jumped around shaking my hand. After that I was more careful and when it happened, I just hissed through my teeth and kept working. Now I knew where Mr. P. had got his fingers.

This was not a career I was going to pursue. I knew that after two days on the job. I couldn't see myself slinging mortar when I was Mr. P.'s age. I wasn't selling refrigerators, either. My old man's hands were okay, but he was always drinking Peptobismol or popping Divol. When he didn't move a refrigerator or a stove for a couple of days, I could hear him walking around the kitchen at night.

Mr. P. showed me a few tricks. I got the mortar so it was the right consistency. It wasn't like this was nuclear science or anything. When someone showed you how to do it, it was pretty easy to get it right.

I was doing okay until Mr. P. told me to build a section that had fallen down. Watching him, I figured there wasn't much to it. I pulled away the rocks so I could see what was left on the bottom. I was lucky because there were two rows of stones still in place. I mixed up a batch of mortar and threw it on the spot where I wanted to begin. I put a stone in place, then another one. I got six stones up, but I could see it wasn't working. The walls had to be vertical and my stones were in and out. I was worried that the mortar was going to set. Then I'd have to hammer it out.

I hated doing it, but I went to where Mr. P. was slapping up a piece of wall.

"I can't do it," I said. I hated that. I hated every word. I didn't want to have to ask anybody for anything but it wasn't like an essay. You couldn't B.S. your way through it. Any dimwit going by could see my stones weren't set right.

Mr. P. finished what he was doing and came to take a look. He took down the stones, then dug around in the dirt until he had a handful of granite shims. He fitted them in place, then balanced the stone. Then he motioned for me to dig around and find shims. When I had some, he got me to put some in place, then set the stone. He did one more, then I did one while he watched. He also added more mortar so the bed was deeper.

After that, he kept an eye on me, and if he saw I couldn't figure something out, he'd come over, watch for awhile, then show me how to do it. After he showed me, he wouldn't leave the stones in place. He set them, then took them down and made me do it over.

My father wanted to make the job into some type of transcendental experience. It wasn't. I wasn't built for this work. I was small and slight. It was the same at school. I had a hard time in the halls and on the parking lot. There were guys who wanted me to pay a toll. One time when I said I wasn't paying, two of them hung me upside down by the ankles and shook me until all my money fell out of my pockets. I'd tried to tell my old man that it wasn't like when he was going to school in Mosquito Creek, Saskatchewan. A hundred kids and all of them had gone to school together since grade one.

Gisli had a bad time at school, too. Neither of us fitted in. I don't know why. Everybody had a group except me and Gisli, so we were our own group.

By the end of the summer, I was pretty good at stacking up rocks. Mr. P. and I got along okay but we weren't buddies. When it came time to say goodbye, he didn't give me his lunch bucket or anything. Instead, he looked me in the eye and said, "Lots of wall still to do. You wanna come back, you can do some more."

It wasn't like it was heaven at home, but the folks had been going to some counselor so they were talking again. It made it easier to hang around the house. My old man took me down to where he worked and showed me around the back. There was just an office and stuff stacked up in boxes waiting to go onto the floor. There was this blackboard calendar with the month and all their names on it and every day the boss wrote in how much each guy had sold. At the end of the month it was added up and the person who had the lowest total got fired.

My folks were on at me about making friends and finding something to do. I told them about the way it was at school. Some people were big wheels and everybody followed them like sheep. I wasn't a big wheel and I wasn't into being a sheep. Maybe that's just the way it was for some people. Like the Sand Sifter. He was always on his own. People stopped and talked to him and everything, but you were never going to see him marching with the Shriners.

I told them he had a second-hand machine for sale. My old man went down with me to meet him. Bert—that was his real name—and my old man got onto how lousy the economy was and how the government was the pits. They talked logging for a bit, then Bert agreed to sell me his old detector. My old man said he'd pay for it up front but he got everything I found until it was paid for. It wasn't a Tesoro Lobo Super Traq but it would do. I had to promise Bert I would find my own places to search.

I hadn't seen Gisli all summer. That was one of the rules when the judge gave us diversion. I drifted past his place twice. I figured we might accidently bump into each other.

The second time I saw no drapes on the windows and a For Rent sign on the lawn. On the first day of school, I checked the halls but he wasn't around, so I went down to the main office and asked what classes he was in. The secretary said he wasn't there.

A couple of weeks later I was down at the harbor listening to The Cockroaches, a South American band with an attitude, when I saw him. He was sitting against the sea wall with his cap in front of him.

"Remember that day I was chucking rocks at Bernardo?" he said after I sat down beside him. "The old man called that morning and told my mom that he didn't want me coming to Calgary. There wasn't room for both me and my sister."

Maybe if I hadn't been thinking so much about burgers and fries that day, things might have been different. Maybe if I'd have been listening. It's hard to know. During the summer, his mom got a boyfriend and they wanted a fresh start. They gave him a fifty and left him on a street corner. That isn't right, you know. Kids have got to have a place. When I saw him, he was living with five other kids in an apartment in James Bay.

There's no happy ending. My English teacher's okay. He likes to talk about things. He says there's fifteen hundred kids in this school. There's never going to be jobs for some of them. There's going to be lousy jobs for lots of them. There's going to be good jobs for a few of them. What's it going to be? No burgers for some, nothing but burgers for others whether they want them or not, and a whole menu for the few. Am I going to get some qualifications or not?

I told him, I'll think about it.

Mrs. Galoshers

Jeremy took a can of apricots off the grocery store shelf. His mother shook her head.

Jeremy sighed. He loved canned fruit. Apricots, peaches, cherries, pears. Fruit salad. It was going to be a long winter without a cupboard full of canned fruit that he could raid. Reluctantly, he put the can back.

Because it was cheaper to live in the country, they'd moved from the city after school finished in June. His father had been laid off but had found part-time work in Eddyville. They couldn't find a house to rent in town, so they'd had to take a place ten miles north in the village of Borg. It was a white frame house that had been sitting empty for awhile. The yard was large and overgrown. His father said the best thing about it was that it was inexpensive, because it wasn't like he had a real job with a salary and benefits. Instead, he was going to do payrolls and books for a variety of small businesses. His territory covered a large area. Sometimes he would have to be away for two or three days at a time.

"At least it's not a farm house," Jeremy had said. When they were house hunting, they'd looked at a number of farm houses. Most of them had no more than one neighbor within a mile. His mother had rebelled. "I'm not living back of beyond," she'd said. "I'm no pioneer." Until they moved to Borg, she'd never been outside the city limits. When she'd found out they were moving to the country, she'd bought a map. From her questions, you'd have thought they were going to darkest Africa instead of seventy miles into the Manitoba countryside.

"No cable," she said. "No taxis. Two cafes in summer. One menu. Apple pie with ice cream and ice cream with apple pie. In winter, one cafe."

Later that morning, Jeremy leaned over their fence. Next door, Mrs. Galoshers was picking beans into an enamel wash basin. Without stopping, she said, "Got to get ready for winter." Her garden took up most of her back yard. There were things in it that Jeremy had never heard of. Kohlrabi, acorn squash, purple beans.

Jeremy knew that Mrs. G. didn't approve of his mother. She particularly didn't approve of his mother's shoes. "City shoes," she sniffed one day just after they'd moved in. "Good for dancing. No good for working."

Mrs. G. was as big as a house, as wide as a mountain, as strong as an ox. She was always digging or weeding or hoeing. She always wore an old pair of galoshes that were never done up. You could hear the sound of the rubber sides flapping as she walked.

"We always lived in an apartment," Jeremy said, defending his mother.

"I lived in apartment one time. I had garden on roof."

Mrs. G. waved her arm at a chicken that had got free from its pen and had wandered into the pea patch. It squawked and fluttered away. When Mrs. G. wanted chicken soup, she grabbed a chicken by the feet, chopped its head off on her chopping block, then plucked it and cleaned it right there.

"Gross," his mother said. "I prefer mine in plastic wrap."

Mrs. G. pulled up some beets and gave them to Jeremy. When she saw him eyeing them suspiciously, she said, "Good for borscht." Their beets always came out of a can. Two minutes in the microwave and they were ready. "No chirp, chirp here. Just ants."

"She talks funny," Jeremy said to his mother, laying the beets on the kitchen counter. He repeated what Mrs. G. had said.

"The grasshopper and the ant," his mother explained. "She's the ant and we're the grasshoppers. We play all day and are frivolous while she works all day and is industrious. She doesn't hold us in high esteem."

"It's your red shoes," Jeremy said. "She thinks they're frivolous."

"As soon as we have some extra money, I'll be sure to order a pair of galoshes from Sears."

Jeremy smiled. The idea of his mother in galoshes was ridiculous. She had a pair of short blue rubber boots for when it rained, but they were quite fashionable and were just meant to keep her feet dry while she walked from the car to the house.

Jeremy thought about digging a garden, but he just couldn't imagine his mother wearing overalls, leaning on a hoe. She was small and blonde. She wore dresses that floated in the breeze. When she was younger, she'd worked for a furrier and modeled coats. She was, he had to admit, Queen of the Can Opener. Deli was one of her favorite words. Back in the city, she'd send Jeremy to the store and say, "Buy something nice at the deli but not so we know where it comes from." Every time she heard a chicken squawk and Mrs. Galosher's ax thunk into the chopping block, she flinched.

One afternoon his father took him and his mother to Eddyville. She went shopping. Jeremy went fishing at the dock for two hours. He didn't catch anything, but a girl gave him two pickerel and told him to use minnows instead of metal spoons. He got a plastic bag from a grocery store and put the fish in the trunk. When she saw the fish, his mother said, "One day we will return to civilization and soda water." She knew all about place settings and folding napkins, but live, flopping fish were out of her realm.

Jeremy took the fish to Mrs. Galoshers.

Mrs. G. went inside for a long, thin knife that she sharpened on a stone. "You watch," she said. She filleted the first fish, then gave the knife to Jeremy. "Now, you do."

Gross, he thought, as he put his hand around the fish. He turned it on its back. He gritted his teeth and sawed with the knife. He managed to get the head off and slit the belly. He cleaned the fish, then looked helplessly at Mrs. G. She took the fish and showed him, once again, how to run the knife along the spine, then strip off the skin. She gave him the other side to do.

The fish slipped and slid and the fillet wasn't nice and smooth like the other three, but it was a fillet.

"I help you. Tomorrow you help me," Mrs. G. said. "Now you take to Tzarina." That, Jeremy realized, was a put-down. Mrs. G. had no use for royalty, particularly not Russian royalty.

"Two channels," his mother complained. "Your father should be working for the government. We'd get a hardship allowance." She was making a shirt for his father. She'd learned a lot about sewing and tailoring at the furrier.

Normally she liked watching soap operas while she sewed.

Jeremy's father was passionate about bridge and chess. When he was home, the three of them played bridge with a dummy hand. Every night before bed, he and Jeremy played one game of chess.

"Made any friends?" his dad asked. Jeremy shook his head. "That's all right. Once school starts, you'll get to know the kids in your class. Try hanging around at the beach."

Jeremy had already tried that. It just meant sitting by himself. Most kids lived on the surrounding farms and they didn't have time to spend at the beach. And even though the cottage owners patronized the local businesses, the locals never mixed with the people they called campers.

"Not much interface," Jeremy said to his dad. "I walked around looking at the cottages. Most of them are way more expensive than the houses." He wondered how his dad was going to do in his sports jackets, white shirts and ties. Jeremy had never seen any local wearing a white shirt or a tie except on Sunday. No preppy clothes, either. It was all blue jeans, overalls, checked shirts and caps that said things like John Deere or United Grain Growers.

He'd like to have made friends, but it wasn't the same as the city where he could go to the park and take out the three-foot chess pieces, set them up for a game and then wait for a challenger. He wasn't really sure what kids did here. There was no rec center. In the winter there was an outdoor skating rink but if people wanted to curl or skate inside, they had to drive to Eddyville. When he'd first seen Eddyville, he'd thought it was a small country town. Now he looked forward to going there because it was so much bigger than Borg.

The next morning, Jeremy climbed over the fence to Mrs. G.'s yard. He hoped they weren't going to be killing chickens.

She set him to work digging potatoes. There were two kinds, white and red. While he dug, she tied garlic into strings. She showed him how to spread the potatoes on a plastic tarp to dry. When he had finished, she brought out bowls of borscht and chicken sandwiches. For dessert, she had poppy seed cake.

"Better than microwave?" she said, and he had to agree.

After they had eaten, she gave him ten dollars and a bag of potatoes.

"Don't buy galoshes with it," his mother said. "That woman wears the same clothes every day. Does she never wash them?"

"She told me when she likes something, she buys six pairs."

"Style," his mother said. "Ain't it grand? Certainly cuts down on making decisions about what you're going to wear."

These were hard times for his mom, Jeremy thought. She used to love getting dressed up and going to the symphony concerts and the theater. She was always flitting around the lobby talking to all the people she knew from the clothing business.

They'd lived downtown in an apartment. He could walk out the door and everything was right there. He could catch a bus to the park or the shopping mall or the swimming pool. Saturdays he often went with his friends to The Forks to skateboard. Downtown everything was moving all the time—police cars, ambulances, traffic—rushing here, rushing there. The city had a rhythm. Sometimes in summer they'd sit on the balcony and listen to the traffic. His father said you could hear the heart of the city beating.

Jeremy hung around the house, sitting on the front porch. Then he walked around the village. A lot of the yards had caragana hedges. There were lots of spruce trees. Most yards had flower gardens in front and vegetable gardens in back. There was a tennis court but it belonged to the campers. They also had a small clubhouse with a juke box. None of the locals ever went there. Some of the yards had boats in them. Some had nets hanging on poles.

Downtown Borg was one block leading to the lake and one block parallel to the lake. Jeremy looked in the windows of the dry goods store, the grocery store, the combined barber shop and beauty parlor. At the far end of the street there was a tailor's shop. The tailor also did shoe repairs. The door was open and Jeremy stood there for a few minutes breathing in the smell of the leather.

The permanent houses were grouped around the downtown. The cottages took up most of the lakefront. They were surrounded by trees. He hoped that he'd see some kids he knew from the city.

Cars were lined up along the beach. The sounds of people laughing and talking rose and fell in waves. He walked along the sand looking at the families gathered under umbrellas and having their lunch at the wooden picnic tables. He wished that he were back at the city pool. He could smell the sharpness of the chlorine, hear the echo of everyone splashing and yelling. He'd be having water fights with his friends.

On the way home he walked along the back lanes. In some yards people were working in their gardens. He was passing a wooden fence when a man dropped an armload of gladioli into the lane. Jeremy stopped to stare. The stalks were every color—red, pink, yellow, orange. He was still standing there staring at the flowers when the man dropped another armload into the lane.

Jeremy wanted to take some but he wasn't sure if it would be all right. Finally he went to the fence and peered between the boards. The man was busy cutting off more spikes.

Jeremy's mother was always telling him he had to quit being so shy, that it wasn't going to kill him to speak to people. She was always introducing him. This is Jeremy, she'd say. He's a very interesting young man. He knows a lot about bridge and chess.

When the man dumped more flowers over the fence, Jeremy worked up his courage and said, "Excuse me. Would it be all right if I took some flowers?" He felt his face flush. He hated that. He always felt his ears were going to catch fire. They were the biggest ears in the world and they turned as red as traffic lights.

"Sure," the man said. "You're the new people that moved into the old Taylor place?"

"Yes," Jeremy admitted. "My mom really likes flowers."

"Help yourself," the man said. "My name's Thompson and I grow flowers for competitions. These are the rejects."

Jeremy said thanks. As he stacked flowers, he couldn't see anything wrong with them. When he had as many as he could carry, he put both arms around them. He had such an armload that he couldn't see straight ahead. He had to keep his eyes on the side of the lane. When he arrived home, he kicked on the bottom of the door.

"What?" his mother said as she opened the door.

"Flowers," Jeremy said. He dumped them on the kitchen table. "Mr. Thompson gave them to me. For free."

When he was seven, Jeremy brought his mother a bouquet. Shortly after there was a knock on the door. It was the vegetable and fruit man. Jeremy had made up the bouquet from the buckets on the sidewalk. His mother paid for the flowers and explained to Jeremy that he had to pay for things.

Mothers, he knew, were like elephants. They never forgot anything you ever did.

They used up all the vases, then the jugs and, finally, some large tin cans. When they were finished, there were flowers in every room.

"Can't eat flowers," Mrs. G. said when he came out the back door. "You want flowers, you grow marigolds to keep off bugs. You gonna dig garden for me?"

She showed him how to double dig the potato patch. Then he cleaned out her compost box and spread the compost. She paid him twenty dollars. "I thought you lazy when I first seen you. Now you know how to dig, you dig garden for your mother. You dig now, it'll be ready by spring."

He had a feeling he was taking some kind of test, except he wasn't sure what it was. She showed him how to clean off the spade and sharpen it. She explained about measuring, putting in corner sticks and string. As he worked, she came and watched over the fence every so often.

"What are you doing?" his mother asked.

"Double digging," he said.

"We're not having chickens," she replied. "I draw the line at chickens."

The next Sunday Mrs. G. saw him in the yard. "My friend need garden dug," she said. "You charge her fifteen dollars. She's on old age pension. Not on pension, you charge twenty. You got nice shirt. You bought with money I pay you?"

"No," he said. He'd told his mother that he wanted a checked shirt like the ones the men in the garage wore. "My mother made it. She can make anything. She makes her own dresses."

Mrs. G. told him to pull his shirt tails out so she could check the seams. She didn't say anything except "Hmmph!"

Mrs. G. kept finding him jobs to do but they were all for people on pensions. None of them had any kids his age. He cut grass for one, did some digging for another. When he wasn't doing some job or other, he drifted down to the beach. Every time he went, he promised himself that he'd go up to some kids and say hello. He always chickened out.

Finally he saw a boy with a medicine ball and no one to throw it back and forth with. He put out his arms as if to catch the ball. The boy threw him the ball. They played catch for awhile, then went swimming together. Afterwards, they had a soft drink and sat on the sand together.

"Do you live here?" Jeremy asked.

Peter shook his head. "Just down for three days. We're using my aunt's cottage."

"I used to go to Balfour," Jeremy said. "You know Balfour?"

"Yeah," Peter replied. "I've been there to play soccer. I go to Kingsway."

Jeremy had been to Kingsway for a chess tournament. They spent an hour talking about the places they both knew. For the next two days Jeremy stopped by Peter's cottage. They hung around the beach.

After Peter left, Jeremy decided that he

wasn't going to make friends with any other cottage kids. It just made things worse. He ended up feeling more lonely and, instead of forgetting about the city, he was thinking about it all the time.

His father was home for a few days. He had a lot of paperwork to do. The three of them went over the budget. Jeremy knew his parents were trying to be democratic by including him, but he wished they wouldn't. He didn't want to know how every penny was spent and how much they had to have to pay the bills. He offered to give them the money he'd made from his odd jobs, but they said he should keep it for spending money since they couldn't afford an allowance.

"There's a theater company," Jeremy said as they were having supper. While he was exploring, he'd read all the notices in the store windows.

"There's no theater," his mother said.

"It's in Eddyville. It's in the old church. The restored one with the spire. They're looking for people to help put on a new play."

"Maybe you could help with costumes, Agnes," his father said. "I doubt if there's anyone around who knows as much about clothes as you. You can probably get a ride in on weekdays and I'll be home on weekends so you can use the car."

Jeremy's mother didn't say yes, but she didn't say no, either.

Later, when they were playing chess, his father said, "It's hard on your mother. I've got my work. You're going to have school. There are no jobs here for her. I know she wants to move back but I think we're going to be here for awhile. I've picked up some more accounts."

Jeremy used some of the money he'd earned to buy canned apricots. He also bought some fresh peaches and cherries from a man who'd parked his truck at the side of the road and put up a sign saying B.C. FRUIT.

In the city when they wanted fruit, they went to a wholesale/retail fruit store. The store had everything. Star fruit, mangoes, papaya, leechee nuts, fresh nuts in burlap sacks, six kinds of pears and apples. Croatian, Russian, Jewish, Trinidadian, African, Ukrainian, East Indian and German accents swirled around the store.

Mrs. G. beckoned to him one day. "I need help," she said. He climbed over the fence. "Getting ready for winter." She was sharpening her ax. He thought she was going to ask him to chop wood for her. She had a wood heater in her living room. "You catch chicken."

Jeremy was startled, but after a moment's hesitation, he ran after one of the chickens that was pecking at the ground. The chickens, which normally seemed hardly to move, suddenly scattered. Bent over with his hands out, he ran after one, then another.

Mrs. G. motioned him back, lifted a finger for him to pay attention. She reached into the pot where she kept the grain. She dribbled some onto the ground. The chickens that had just run away came running back. In one quick move, she swept her hand underneath one, grabbing it by the feet. She carried it over to the chopping block and cut off its head. Jeremy shut his eyes.

"Can't catch with eyes shut," she said.

It took him three tries, but then he had one. He caught twenty. Mrs. G. kept chucking the bodies into a washtub. She got him to help her carry out a tub of scalding hot water. They dipped the chickens into it to loosen the feathers. Then they began to pluck. When the plucking was done, she showed him how to clean one of the chickens, then left him to it.

The first time he put his hand into a chicken's body cavity, he understood why his mother preferred things from the deli that were not identifiable.

"You did what?" his mother said. He was standing in the kitchen with a chicken in one hand and ten dollars in the other. She was convinced that he was going to need therapy for the rest of his life.

"She's going to can them. I didn't know you could can chickens. I mean, we bought them in cans in the city but I didn't know just anybody could can them."

"I'm going to become a vegetarian before this is over," his mother replied. That night she got him to read some poetry by Tennyson. "When things are better, we'll go to the ballet and have lunch at the art gallery," she promised.

She drove to a meeting at the Eddyville theater and volunteered to help with costumes. She came home and started drawing pictures of what the costumes might look like. Jeremy sighed with relief. Adults found it so hard to adapt sometimes. Still, he had some idea how they felt. One day everything seemed normal and predictable. You had a life. Then some company you'd never heard of bought your company and you got a pink slip. He thought it must be like when there was an earthquake and the ground turned to liquid. One moment you were on solid ground and the next you were sinking. His dad had said it was going to be a long winter for them.

Jeremy leaned on the fence and looked at the remains of Mrs. G.'s garden. There was still a lot to harvest. He thought about her full shelves and their empty shelves. It wasn't that they were grasshoppers. They knew how to work, but they worked at different things. If Mrs. G. was forced to move to the city, she wouldn't have got a job modeling at the furrier's. Jeremy chuckled to himself. He could just imagine what it would be like to see Mrs. G. strutting down the ramp in her galoshes.

He figured that since he was going to be living in Borg for at least a year, he might as well go exploring. Bike riding was better than sitting around wishing he was still in the city.

He took the dirt road out of town. The trees were gray with dust. At last he came to an open field with some cows and large piles of old brush. He saw something red in the bushes along the fence. When he bent down to look, he saw they were raspberries.

When he had finished eating them, he reached through the fence to pick some more. He realized that raspberry canes were growing around one of the piles. The cows had moved off to stand under some scrubby poplar trees, so he climbed through the fence to get a better look. The bushes were covered in raspberries.

He ate until he'd eaten all he wanted, and then he jumped on his bike and raced home.

"Mom, Mom," he shouted as he barged through the door. "I've found raspberries. Lots of them."

"We can pick some," she said, "but they don't keep. They get moldy pretty quickly."

"Can them," he said.

"I don't know how to can."

"Never mind," he said. "We'll figure it out." He rummaged under the sink, collecting plastic buckets. "Two buckets each. One for each handlebar."

His mother changed into slacks, grabbed her straw hat with the blue ribbon and followed him down the steps.

When they got to the field, his mother said, "That's a bull. It's got horns."

"It's a cow," Jeremy replied. "Cows have horns, too." His mother didn't look convinced. "You can't milk a bull. You can milk her."

They filled their buckets. They rode home, emptied out their berries and went back and picked more berries. They made three trips.

"Garnets," Jeremy said. "Rubies, red diamonds."

"Don't exaggerate. It makes people's blood pressure go up. Your uncle Harry always exaggerated and he died of a stroke." Jeremy's mother studied the berries. "Now what do we do?"

Jeremy ran to get Mrs. Galoshers.

"Berries!" he said.

She came thumping behind him. "Holy moly," she said. "You got some sealers?"

Jeremy's mother shook her head.

"I got extra. You come with me."

Jeremy helped carry over boxes of sealers. They carried over the big blue canner. They brought a sack of sugar. Mrs. Galoshers started them washing jars. She began to boil up a sugar syrup. Then they cleaned the berries, getting rid of leaves and twigs and the occasional spider.

They sterilized the jars. Then they packed them. Mrs. Galoshers poured in the hot syrup, then sealed the jars. They put them in the canner. When one batch was done, they put another batch on the stove. They worked all evening and until late in the night. Finally, surrounded by jars, they were finished. Their hands were stained red right to the wrists.

"I come back in morning," Mrs. G. said. She took a third of the raspberries. Jeremy fell asleep on top of his bed with his clothes still on.

Mrs. G. woke him up knocking on the door. Jeremy staggered into the kitchen. All night long, he'd dreamt he was picking raspberries.

His mother was already up washing the pots and pans. The cupboard and kitchen table were covered with jars of preserved raspberries.

"You show me," Mrs. G. said to Jeremy. They got into her old Pontiac. They picked berries all morning.

"Some people see no-good field, some people see opportunity," Mrs. Galoshers said when they came back. They were sitting in her kitchen having a glass of lemonade. "Your mom, she's gonna make a garden next year. You wanna bet? I'm going to wedding. Maybe she will make me dress. Better than from catalog."

There would be no problem about the dress, Jeremy knew. His mother could make one without even using a pattern. But he couldn't quite envision Mrs. G. in a dress. He wondered if she'd wear her galoshes.

Cabin Fever

"I really wish you'd come to the Stewarts with us," Annie Lee's mother said.

"I've got lots to do," Annie Lee replied.

"I'll bet Stella has made a pan of brownies just for you."

"I've got homework and things," Annie Lee said vaguely. "You know."

They were doing it again, she thought. Avoiding the real subject. She wondered if they'd ever start talking about things directly, just saying what was on their minds instead of always approaching everything from an angle. It was if they were afraid to say the wrong thing.

"Leave her alone, Jane," Annie Lee's father said. "It's the Age of Moods. Don't you remember?"

She saw her mother tip her head back stiffly.

She did that when her feelings were hurt.

"I'll be fine," Annie Lee repeated, trying to reassure them. "Cross my heart."

"I'm just trying to help."

Her mother was right, of course. She made a career out of being right. Mrs. Stewart would have a pan of brownies sitting on the cupboard. Mr. and Mrs. Stewart would both ask her how school was going. Then the adults would leave her to read old copies of National Geographic while her father pumped Mr. Stewart for information he could use in his dissertation. Annie Lee's father was taking a year off teaching so he could finally finish his doctorate. If he didn't get it done he wasn't going to get tenure, and if he didn't get tenure he was going to lose his job, and if he lost his job they were going to have to move, and if they had to move, Annie Lee's mother was going to go nuclear.

Her father was hoping that he could get Mr. Stewart to tell him about the abandoned church that sat on the Stewarts' land. It was tiny. No more than twelve people could crowd into it. It was built in the old Icelandic style, with low stone walls topped with turf and a steep roof.

The last time they'd visited the Stewarts, Annie Lee had circled the church three times. It was made of unpainted boards that were black with age. The roof was steep and the shingles were thick with moss.

She finally worked up her courage and pushed open the front door. To her surprise there was a pulpit and a nave. There were four pews that could seat three people each. The pews were mottled with colored light from the windows. On the ends of the pews were the remnants of paper flowers. At one time the paper had been red and blue, but over the years it had faded, so that when she stretched the stiff petals there were only traces of color in the deepest creases. There were black hymnals in the holders attached to the back of the pews. She opened one. She couldn't read it because it was in Icelandic. She climbed the three steps into the pulpit.

All at once Annie Lee had shivered. It felt as if someone else was there, watching her. She'd backed away and hurried outside. Dark clouds had gathered, and the overgrown churchyard with its tangle of undergrowth and gravestones was thick with shadows. She'd run all the way back to the house.

Now she shivered once again. Although sunlight streamed through the windows and the sky was bright blue, it was as if she could still feel the weight of those gray clouds.

Annie Lee looked at her father. He shuffled uncomfortably. "She'll be fine, Jane. Won't you, honey? She just needs some time to herself. We're all suffering a bit from cabin fever."

"Fine," her mother said. But she said it in that tight-voiced way she had when she felt something wasn't fine at all.

Before Annie Lee's parents left, her father gave her three warnings about bears. No leaving food on the picnic table. No frying bacon with the door open. No going for a hike unless she had a can with some pebbles in it that she could shake to let everything know she was coming.

"You'll be home by supper time," she replied, trying to reassure them. "If I want a snack, I'll make a peanut butter and jam sandwich."

"I just thought you'd like to get out of the house," her mother said. She never gave up. No wonder she was good at collecting bills. She was the top bill collector at the finance company where she worked.

"Next time," Annie Lee said.

Five days a week she traveled that road in the school bus. Now that the ground was no longer frozen, she always arrived at school covered in dust from the crushed limestone surface. The first few times she'd seen the tamarack forest, the muskeg, the creeks with the beaver dams, the scattered, mostly abandoned farmhouses, the trip had been interesting. After a week, she'd quit paying attention.

She was the oldest kid on the bus. At first she tried sitting at the back, but the boys spent their time wrestling and punching each other and stealing each other's caps. Then she tried the middle of the bus. The little girls squealed and yelled like a flock of demented birds. Finally, she settled on the front where the driver actually kept some control.

Vik wasn't really a town. There were just a dozen houses and four large dormitories for the single workers at the mine. The bus riders were kids living on small farms. Their parents grew grain on ground high enough to be cleared, cut pulp in winter, did some commercial fishing, kept some cows and pigs and chickens. Hard scrabble living was how her mother described it.

Her father stopped at the gate so her mother could call to see if she'd changed her mind. Annie Lee waved for them to keep going. The car turned and disappeared behind the trees. She stood there listening until she couldn't hear the sound of the tires on gravel anymore. It was so quiet she could hear her heart beat. Lub-a-dub, lub-a-dub.

The moment her parents left, she turned up the radio and began to dance. She danced with her eyes shut, remembering what her old jazz dance classes had been like, remembering the last school dance where the music had made the walls vibrate, enclosing her in an ocean of sound. She danced until she could feel sweat begin to form between her shoulder blades.

As she danced, she suddenly thought, "I hope they never come back." Then, shocked, she snapped open her eyes and thought, "No, I don't mean that." It was like a ghostly part of herself ran after the thought, chasing it down the driveway and onto the road, trying to catch it before it reached its destination.

She changed stations and danced more quietly then, moving in slow circles around the room. Finally, she fell into the chair and waited for the sense that her ghost self had returned. When that didn't happen, she put on her boots and jacket and went outside.

When they'd lived in the city, there had always been noise. Buses went right past their place. All day, all night. When they went back for two weeks at Christmas so her father could do some research in the archives, Annie Lee couldn't sleep because of the constant noise. The traffic slowed down around three A.M., but it never stopped. There was always a siren starting up somewhere, an occasional plane, someone yelling or laughing. She wondered why, when they'd lived in the city, she hadn't noticed the cacophony.

When they moved to Vik, it was just the opposite. For the first few nights, she couldn't sleep because it was so quiet. When an owl hooted, a wolf howled, the wood in the stove crackled, she didn't just hear it with her ears but with her skin, with her tongue, with her eyes.

One time she told her father that a crow cawing smelled slightly bitter, like freshly cut poplar. She'd seen his startled, worried look and now she didn't tell him that sort of thing anymore. The psychologist she'd talked to before they moved to Vik had explained to her it was like she had super-sensitive senses. It was as if most people were color blind but she could see color. Trying to explain to them what she saw would be difficult. That was one of the reasons that she often felt lonely.

Since they'd moved to Vik the past summer, she had adjusted to the silence, the moods of the lake, the brooding darkness of the forest. Her parents had brought a TV, but after a day of climbing onto the roof and adjusting an aerial, her father had given up trying to make it work. No matter how many times he moved the aerial, all they got were some ghostly, unidentifiable images and a screen so filled with snow that it looked like a blizzard. They were able to make use of the TV and VCR because the hotel on the other side of the lake rented videos. The bus driver always stopped so the kids could take back videos and rent new ones.

They all were having to adjust. Maybe because there was no escaping each other her father had started to pay more attention to her. In the fall they'd tried fishing. During the winter they'd gone cross-country skiing. They'd even tried snowshoeing. Lately, as the weather had improved, the two of them had played a silly game of ice walking. The goal was to see who could go the farthest without breaking through the ice. They always stayed close to shore where the water was no more than knee deep.

Annie Lee took a book and a blanket down to the shingle beach. The gray and white stones were the size and shape of mangoes. Behind the beach were low limestone cliffs. High water and ice were constantly breaking away sections, leaving pillars and nooks. Inside one of these nooks she and her father had put a piece of plywood big enough to lie on. They'd fitted aluminum foil over the surrounding layers of limestone and called the space their suntanning room.

She took off her jacket and stretched out in the heat. The icy surface of the lake was covered with shallow pools of water. In some places the ice would be thick and solid, but in other places it would be dangerously thin. Some of the fishermen had dragged an old car onto the ice. In the hotel cafe they'd tacked up a piece of cardboard on which you could choose the day and the hour when the car would fall through the ice. Each guess cost a dollar. The dollars were put in a pickle jar on the counter. Whoever won got the pickle jar full of loonies.

Living at Vik had changed everything. Her father wasn't going off to teach every day. Her mother wasn't rushing out in the morning, throwing supper together in the evening, then dashing off to sell jewelry at house parties. In the city they'd all ricocheted off each other and everything else. She'd been ricocheting, too. Off to school. Off to drama classes. Off to soccer. Off to dance classes. Off to figure skating. Off, off, off, off.

Her father spent more time with her now. Before it was like he'd be surprised to notice her. She sometimes wondered if she shouldn't introduce herself to him. "Hi, I'm Annie Lee. I'm your daughter. I live here, too." Her mother was different. She moved at the speed of light. It was impossible to ask her a question because she was gone before the question was finished. Zoom. Zoom. Superwoman flashing past. After they moved to Vik, her mother was confused. It took her awhile to realize that she could watch a movie without simultaneously writing reports on her laptop.

The psychologist had also talked to Annie Lee's parents. That was why her dad had read a book on fishing and bought two rods so they could fish from the shore. She could see, though, how awkward and uncertain he was, and that made her nervous. Dads were supposed to know everything. What he knew about were sources and footnotes for folktales and myths. He'd been reading books on parenting. She just wished that when they went for a hike and he pointed out a beaver or hawk there wasn't such a desperate look in his eyes. She wanted to tell him that he could go back to his trolls and goblins and giants, that she was fine, that there was nothing to worry about.

Except she couldn't say that because she didn't know. Sometimes her mind and body still drifted apart. Not far apart, not like when her mind floated to the far corner of the room and watched her body wandering around. That hadn't happened for awhile.

When they first came to Vik, her mother's cellular was Annie Lee's lifeline. Every Sunday night she called her friends in the city. At first an hour wasn't enough time. Now it was too much. As the months passed, there was less and less to talk about.

She'd made one trip back but it had been a disaster. Rhonda, one of her classmates at the Vik school, had asked Annie Lee if she'd like to go to the city with her and her parents. Annie Lee arranged to meet some friends from the year before at a mall. When they met, she wanted to tell them about the bear that had raided the garden, the moose that wouldn't let the school bus pass, the visit underground at the mine. Her former friends kept talking about who had the widest pant legs. After fifteen minutes they said it was nice seeing her but they had to meet their boyfriends.

She thought they'd never see anyone after they moved, but it wasn't like that at all. Someone was always dropping by. Most of the time it was local people who were on their way to or from the city. No one ever called ahead. Her mother had adjusted to people announcing their arrival by tooting their horns three or four times, then coming in to visit. Her mother always put the coffee pot on. Occasionally, game wardens or other government workers stopped by. A couple of times friends and relatives came for a weekend.

Annie Lee was lying with her eyes closed when she suddenly felt chilly. She shivered and looked up. When she'd come out, the sky had been clear. Now, clouds were gathering. As she watched, a high white thunderhead formed, then turned dark. She could see the wind before it reached her. As it came scudding in her direction, the thin layer of water on the ice rippled.

Storms came up fast here. She'd seen it happen before. The sun would be shining, the sky blue. Then a storm would come racing across the lake so fast there'd barely be time to get your line out of the water before the wind struck.

Annie Lee picked up her book and went inside. She put a piece of birch into the stove, then made herself a sandwich. She hoped it wasn't going to rain. The road wasn't paved, and when it got wet it became slippery and dangerous.

Shortly after that the rain started. She made herself a sandwich and lay down on the couch to read. In the midst of Lady Gertrude being rescued by the handsome Sir Richard, the rhythm of the rain on the roof put her to sleep.

When she woke up, the ruts leading to the road were full of water. A large puddle covered most of the yard. Annie Lee pulled on her mother's old slicker, then took a shovel and dug a small channel so the water would drain down the slope into the lake.

Back inside, she checked the clock. Her parents should have been back. They had this fetish about being prompt. Their idea of being on time was to be five minutes early.

An hour later, it was dark. She kept glancing at the clock. She hoped that they hadn't started back after the rain began. If they had, they were probably mired in mud, sunk right to the axels. In the fall even a little rain made the road so slippery that cars often slid into the ditch. Even though truckloads of crushed limestone were dumped every fall, the road sank into the muskeg in the spring. She'd heard stories about how some vehicles sank out of sight.

Annie Lee went to get her mother's cellular so she could phone the Stewarts. It wasn't on the counter. That's when she remembered that there was something wrong with it. Her mother was going to give it to Mr. Stewart so that he could take it into Winnipeg to be repaired.

Outside the window the three windmills she'd made from plastic bleach bottles spun furiously in the wind. That's the way she'd felt about her parents and herself. Windmills turning so fast that one of them ripped right off its foundation and toppled over. Her father was spinning furiously as he taught full time and worked on his doctorate in the evenings and on weekends. Her mother spun furiously as she collected more and more accounts and sold jewelry in the evenings. She was determined to make the Million Dollar Club.

Annie Lee had thought that when people had nervous breakdowns they screamed and yelled and smashed things while they drooled. It hadn't been like that at all. One night her mind and body simply got disconnected. Her mind was here and her body was there. Her mind floated up into a corner of the room and watched as her body opened the medicine cabinet and her hand started to feed her mouth an entire bottle of headache tablets. When her father got home, the empty bottle was lying on the counter and she was lying on the bathroom floor. At the hospital they shoved a hose up her nose and pumped her stomach.

She didn't start to cry until she got home. Then she cried like the rain. She cried until the pillow was soaked, the sheets were drenched, the carpet flooded. At least, that was how it felt. Not noisy crying like she did when she was small and wanted someone to pay attention to her. She cried silently, her body limp, her head buried in the soggy pillow, tears streaming out of her eyes.

"Kids don't have nervous breakdowns," her father said, but he sounded scared. "What's she got to be nervous about? She's got everything. Look at her closet. Hundred-and-twenty-dollar runners."

Then her mother was crying. Between her and her mother, the basement was going to flood. Her father's voice went up an octave. He depended on her mother to be in charge. When she lost control, he panicked.

The next week Annie Lee went to see the psychologist the doctor had recommended. He explained to Annie Lee that trying to be perfect was not a good goal. That's when she told him about the windmills, about how they had to go faster and faster or they wouldn't get enough done.

Annie Lee looked out the window. It was still raining. Her mother was going to be having fits. The year before when they were still living in the city, the smallest thing made her mother worry. Annie Lee was too pale. She was too pink. One of the boys in her class walked her home. Nobody in her class walked her home. She skipped one class to go to the mall and that meant she was on the slippery slope to becoming a juvenile delinquent.

Her mother was probably calling 911, Search and Rescue, and the prime minister's office demanding that something be done immediately. As soon as the clouds disappeared, people would be parachuting down with supplies.

Her father applied for a fellowship so he could take a year off and concentrate on getting his doctorate completed. Her mother arranged for a year's leave of absence. The school gave Annie Lee the average of her year's grades and waived the need for her to take any tests.

Her parents knew that they'd never change

unless they went some place where they couldn't be busy all the time. That's when her father thought about renting a place at Vik. He had lived in the area when he was a boy.

They found a farmhouse that wasn't being used anymore. It turned out that it was owned by the daughter of people who had been friends of his grandparents. He tracked her down. She was living in an old folks' home in Selkirk. Annie Lee and her father drove there to see her.

Miss Ingimundsson had long white hair and wore a long black dress. She sat very straight in her chair and served them tea and biscuits. Annie Lee's father tried to explain how a year's rent would pay for her taxes and insurance. Miss Ingimundsson said she was quite capable of paying the taxes and insurance herself, thank you. Then she turned her attention to Annie Lee. She wanted to know if Annie Lee liked school, what interests and plans she had, what her favorite subjects were. The two of them chattered away like they'd known each other forever.

She sent Annie Lee to the counter to fetch a picture. In it Miss Ingimundsson was standing in front of the farmhouse. Annie Lee knew it had to be a long time ago because the house looked quite new and Miss Ingimundsson looked very young. She had on a long dress with a lot of flounces. She was holding a hat with a wide brim. She had her hair done up in a braid that was pinned to one side.

"Do you see this brooch?" she asked, pointing at the picture. The brooch was pinned between the two sides of the collar.

"It's beautiful," Annie Lee replied.

Miss Ingimundsson got up and went to the bedroom. When she came back she had the brooch in her hand. It was made of silver and had an intricate, delicate pattern. She pinned it to Annie Lee's blouse, then got her to stand in front of the mirror.

"It suits you," she said. "You've got good cheekbones. It gives your face character." She insisted that Annie Lee keep the brooch. "I'm an old woman now," she said. "This is meant for a young woman."

On the way home Annie Lee asked, "Do you think we might be related? We look alike."

Her father shrugged. "Could be," he said. "At one time there were only forty thousand people in all of Iceland. The island has been isolated for centuries. Everybody is related. When I was a kid everybody seemed to be a cousin of some kind."

After they got home, Annie Lee's father told her mother that he thought the only reason Miss Ingimundsson had rented them the place was because of Annie Lee.

She was heating a can of soup when the lights went out. She was so startled that she yelled. Gradually, her eyes adjusted to the dark. She got a flashlight, then hunted for the candles. The matches were beside the stove. She lit three candles and set them on the table. The soup was warm so she ate it right away with some bread and cheese.

The rain was coming down in buckets, like cats and dogs, like frogs and logs. It was like standing at the bottom of Niagara Falls, Annie Lee thought. She was trying to distract herself by thinking of clichés. If the rain kept up, the world was going to disintegrate like saturated newspaper. The ground would turn to bottomless mush. The house would collapse slowly, the walls crumpling. She'd be marooned in a leaky, sinking house. Her parents would sink into the flooded muskeg.

Her mother was always warning her not to wish for things. That morning she'd wanted to have some space for herself. She'd wished that they'd go away and leave the house to her. She hadn't said that she wanted to spend the night alone without a telephone and no electricity.

She put some wood into the stove, then blew out the candles and went to bed.

It was still raining in the morning. The power hadn't come on. Annie Lee used the top of the airtight stove to heat some milk for hot chocolate. She even managed to make toast and scrambled eggs. After breakfast she trudged as far as the road. She sank past her ankles in the gray mud. The ditches on either side were overflowing. In places water streamed across the road. The muddy stream was too thin for a car, her dad would have said, too thick for a boat. The sound of the rain through the trees was a steady sizzling hum.

She had hoped the school bus might come, but she realized as water eddied around her boots that nothing was going to be moving until the rain stopped and the road started to dry.

I never thought I'd want to see the school bus, she thought. She wanted to be there when the car went through the ice. Joan, the owner of the cafe, promised that when the car started to sink, she'd bang on the triangle in front of the hotel. Everybody would come running. They all wanted to be there with their watches ready. All the days were taken up and so were the hours. Some spaces on the calendar were divided into five-minute intervals. The rule was that the car had sunk when the roof disappeared, but there were long arguments about that. Some people thought it should be when the wheels first went down.

Annie Lee read for most of the morning. Then she heated a basin of rainwater and washed her hair. She braided it, trying to make it look like the braids in Miss Ingimundsson's picture. She undid it, then braided it again. She put on her mother's white blouse with the ruffle. She pinned Miss Ingimundsson's brooch at her throat. Every so often she glanced nervously at the sky. She didn't want to spend another night by herself.

She went to make herself more hot chocolate, only to discover that there was a half cup of milk left. Her mother kept canned goods in the old log cabin opposite the farmhouse.

When she opened the door, a horse and rider were coming up the slope from the lake. The horse was a large chestnut with feet the size of small snowshoes. Annie Lee had seen horses like that at the agricultural fair in Brandon. They competed in pulling contests.

The rider had on a jacket of oiled canvas with a hood. When he pulled back the hood, she saw that he was young and had dark, curly hair. He wore dark wool pants and short rubber boots.

A hunk, she thought. The kind of guy you only saw on posters. There was a guy in the high school that looked something like that. Whenever he went by she could feel her heart flutter.

"I've come to get you," he said. "I'm sorry you've had to wait so long."

"Did my parents send you?" she asked.

He nodded. "We need to leave," he said. "We've a long way to go."

"Do you want coffee?" she asked. "You must be cold. I can make you something to eat." He tipped back his head to look at the sky. The clouds were still low and gray.

"We don't have time," he said. "I've come to take you to the other side." He held out his hand, palm up.

She knew he was right. It could start raining heavily again at any moment. She raced back into the house, checked to see that all the appliances were unplugged. If the electricity went on, they wouldn't be ruined by a power surge. Her jacket wouldn't keep her dry in a hard rain, so she pulled her mother's slicker over her shoulders like a cloak.

He lifted her onto the horse, then climbed up behind her. Every time the horse moved on the soft ground, its feet made holes that immediately filled with water.

"What's your name?" she asked.

"Ingthor," he replied.

She expected him to go up the driveway and onto the road. Instead, he turned toward the lake. She wondered if the road was so flooded that he'd detoured down to the lakeshore to get around the worst part.

As the horse picked its way down the crumbling slope, she said, "Are you going to follow the shore, then cut back to the road?"

He didn't answer. The horse stepped onto the ice. Instead of turning, it headed for the opposite shore.

"You're not going to cross the ice?" Annie Lee said sharply. She thought of the car sinking lower into the ice each day. A large horse with two people on it could break through just about anywhere. "You didn't come across the lake, did you?"

"Yes," he said. "I knew you'd been waiting a long time."

Everywhere she looked, the ice was covered with water.

"I don't think I want to do this," she answered. "I think I'll stay here and wait." She went to slide down but he caught her with one arm while he held the bridle with the other. She looked down. Water was splashing from the horse's feet. He tightened his grip, pulling her against him. As the horse began to canter, they rocked back and forth.

"Let me go!" she said. "What do you think you're doing?" She expected him to stop and let her get off. Instead, he urged the horse forward. "There could be open water out there!" She grabbed at the arm that held her and tried to pull it away, but he was as rigid as iron.

"Don't be afraid," he said. "We'll be together."

"Who are you?" she demanded as she struggled. "My parents never sent you."

Unable to move his arm, she twisted sideways inside the slicker. As she turned, she pulled her right leg over the horse.

The horse was beginning to gallop. She was afraid of falling to the ice, afraid of the horse's flying hooves, but she was more afraid of the white, mist-filled world ahead of her. She held her breath and pushed herself away from the horse. Her body slid through the slicker. She fell to the ice and rolled through the cold surface water. She was afraid he would turn around and come back for her. She pushed herself to her feet, then started toward shore, slipping and sliding on the ice. Once she turned to look over her shoulder and saw, to her relief, that the rider and horse were disappearing into the drizzle and mist.

She was soaking wet. Around her she could see where the ice was broken. She ran back, picking out the solid-looking spots, playing the game she'd played with her father many times, but this time aware that if she went through the ice, pulling herself out would be nearly impossible. Twice she felt the ice give, but she sprang forward onto more solid footing. She was shaking with cold as she ran into the house and locked the door behind her.

She was shaking so hard that she could barely get her clothes off. She wrapped herself in a blanket, then shoved wood into the stove. She knew that she had to get something warm to drink. As she filled the kettle with water, her hands shook so much that water splashed all over the cupboard. When the tea was ready, she pressed the mug against her lips to hold it steady so she could take a sip.

She was pulling on her tracksuit when she heard a noise. She stopped and listened. She thought it might be thunder, but then the noise continued. She leaned close to the window. The noise grew louder.

A tractor appeared. It stopped in front of the house.

The driver was dressed in a black norwester. Two people were standing on a hitch at the back. They were wearing bright yellow rain gear and rubber boots. When the tractor pulled up to the door, she realized that the couple in yellow were her mother and father. The tractor turned around immediately. The driver left with a wave of his hand.

When her parents came in, they pulled off their rain gear and gave her a hug. In spite of their waterproof outfits, they were filthy from the mud kicked up by the tractor's wheels. Annie Lee's father went out to split some wood.

"We were worried sick," she said while she drank some of the tea Annie Lee had made. "I'm sorry you were alone all that time. I kept thinking about bears. Your father said no bear would be crazy enough to be out in this weather. He knew you'd be perfectly all right. He kept saying how much common sense you have."

"Did you send anyone to come and get me?" Annie Lee asked.

"Honey, I called all sorts of people. I even called the RCMP. Nobody could do anything. Then we thought about Mr. Wespers. You know his place? He works in the mine but he's also got a tractor for hauling pulpwood in the winter. He brought us as quickly as he could. If it hadn't been for him, we'd still be sitting at the Stewarts."

Later, when Annie Lee and her father were sitting at the kitchen table, he said, "Do you remember Miss Ingimundsson?"

"The old lady?" she replied.

"She died two days ago. Someone called Bob Stewart and told him."

"Did she have any family?"

"I finally got Bob to tell me the story about that little church at the corner of his land. It turns out she was living here with her parents. She was engaged to the young man who lived on the Stewart property. He was a carpenter. They'd wanted to get married for some time but Miss Ingimundsson said that she wasn't going to get married until she could do it properly in a church. So he built her one. When he had it finished, he came to get her. It was around this time of year and the weather was terrible. He started over the ice. He never made it. They never found him or his horse. The current and the ice could have taken them who knows where."

A shiver ran over Annie Lee.

"What's the matter?" her father asked.

"I…" Annie Lee stopped. She didn't want them thinking she'd had another nervous breakdown. After staying so close that she felt they were grafted to her, she didn't want to say anything that would make them think they had to keep watching her. "Nothing. I just went out for wood and slipped and fell. I got soaking wet. What," she asked, "was her fiance's name?"

"Oh, I don't know," he replied. "Next time we're over we can ask Bob. It was one of his relatives. That's how he got the property. Family skeletons. He probably wouldn't have told me anything if I hadn't been there when he got the news."

When her father was researching folk tales and myths he heard a lot of strange stuff. He often said that things happened for which there was no explanation. Not big things like wars, but bits of things like fragments of lives that were left over, that were unfinished. The psychologist explained one time that some people see things that others don't, feel things that others don't. She was supposed to see the psychologist when they moved back to the city. She wasn't sure what she'd tell him.

When she was hanging up her wet clothes, she took Miss Ingimundsson's brooch and went to the window. The temperature had gone up and the lake was shrouded in fog.

Her father was happily typing up the notes he'd made during his visit with the Stewarts. The power was back on and her mother was having a shower. Annie Lee looked around the room. They'd be leaving in a couple of months and then this part of her life would be over. Everything here would just be a memory. The school bus, the hotel cafe, the car on the ice, the lake, this room with her father hunched over his computer, her mother finally letting go enough to take a long shower and to lie around and read a novel afterwards.

She squeezed the brooch, then slipped it into her pocket. She ran her hand over the wooden counter, feeling how smooth it was from the years of use. She took a deep breath. The slightly sharp, sweet smell of burning spruce filled her lungs. The wood cracked with a sharp pop.

The rain had stopped and the fog was glowing. Somewhere out there was her mother's old yellow slicker. Somewhere out there the imprints of a horse's hooves were etched in the melting ice. By the next day they'd be gone.

But, she wondered, peering into the white light, where did they finally lead?

Bush Boy

"Hey, Bush Boy, what're you doing?" Lance called over the noise in the hallway. People were pushing past. Others were opening and closing their lockers. A few of them turned to look at who was doing the yelling.

"Bushby," Jamie replied.

"That's what I said, Bush Boy. What's your old man up to?"

"Picking mushrooms," Jamie said. He didn't like talking about it. Everybody knew his dad had been hurt when a snag fell on him. Snags were called widow makers. They hung up in the branches and could drop on you without warning.

His dad was getting better but he wasn't going to be logging for awhile. When he could, he picked mushrooms and gathered salal. Anything to make a few bucks and to keep busy. There was worker's compensation and Jamie's mom had her job at the grocery store, but they'd explained to him that things were going to be tight for awhile. He'd had his heart set on a dirt bike, but he wasn't going to have one unless he found some way to get it for himself.

Coming from anybody but Lance, being called Bush Boy was good for a punch in the arm. Lance could get away with it because they'd been friends when they were little and lived next door to each other. There was a creek that ran through their backyards, and they spent a lot of time playing together, even though Lance was two years older. Jamie had named himself Bush Boy then. He saw himself as Tarzan of the northern forests. Only Lance knew where the name had come from.

They'd had a tree house and a swing made from a rope and a tire. They'd swing as high as they could and yell at the top of their lungs. Lance had even talked Jamie into jumping off the swing into the creek. He'd broken his ankle that way.

Lance always had great ideas for adventures, but before they were over, Jamie always seemed to be in trouble. There was the time Lance suggested they borrow a rowboat to go crabbing. He forgot to mention that he hadn't asked permission. They both ended up sitting on a bench in the police station until their parents came to get them. That was when Jamie's mother and father suggested he find someone his own age to play with.

His parents weren't unhappy when Lance's family moved to Duncan. They were gone for three years. When they came back, they bought a house on the west side of town. Lance had his own crowd now, and they didn't want someone younger hanging around with them.

Since he'd returned, Lance had been wearing a wool poncho. He had his head shaved on both sides. The rumor was that the stud in his left ear was a real diamond.

"We're going dirt biking," Lance said. "You want to come?"

Jamie knew Lance had a new dirt bike. He and his friends had been racing over the hiking trails. They weren't supposed to because it tore up the thin topsoil and caused the ground to wash away. When someone complained, Lance shrugged it off. "What're you going to do about it? Arrest me?" He knew people would grumble but they wouldn't actually do anything. The local Mountie was busy giving out speeding tickets and reporting accidents.

Jamie desperately wanted to try out Lance's bike. He imagined himself flying over the bumps and sliding around the corners.

Stupid snag, he thought. *Stupid tree. Stupid father for not getting out of the way fast enough.* Then he felt guilty. His dad was lucky he hadn't been standing one step over. The snag would have come right down on top of him instead of just giving him a glancing blow.

The bell was ringing for the last class. The crowd started to thin out as people went to their classrooms.

"No, I'd better pick 'shrooms," he said. "Thanks."

Lance laughed. His two friends laughed with him. They always laughed when Lance laughed. If Lance frowned, they frowned. They walked on each side of him, pushing people in the hall out of the way. Jamie thought of them as Dopey and Grumpy. Their real names were Donald and Gerald.

When Jamie got home, he made himself a

peanut butter and banana sandwich, wrapped it up and put it in his pocket. He added a soft drink and some trail mix. He picked up his white bucket from the garage. He rode out on his bike. The place where he picked was three kilometers out of town. When he got there, he stashed his bike in the bush. Mushroom pickers kept their areas secret. None of them wanted to find a good place and then have someone else come and pick it.

His dad was driving back and forth to Victoria for a few weeks to do physio, so Jamie was on his own. The problem was they hadn't had much rain. The forest was dry and that meant the mushrooms weren't sprouting up like they normally did. Also, Jamie got paid by weight. In dry weather the mushrooms barely weighed anything. In wet weather they were large and heavy.

Unfortunately, there wasn't anything else to do to make money. Once a week he rode his bike up and down the highway, picking up bottles and cans for the refunds. That made him a few dollars but it wasn't steady. Besides, the store would only take forty-eight cans a day. The fact that his mom worked there meant he couldn't try taking in more than the maximum.

Picking mushrooms was hard work. There was no flat area here. Just steep cliffs and ridges. He started just off the roadside, scouring the ground for the light golden color of chanterelles. They were the only mushrooms he picked. There was no making mistakes with chanterelles, his dad said. Nothing else looked like them except the false chanterelle. It sort of looked like a chanterelle, but when you looked at it closely you could see that instead of the smooth shape of the real chanterelle, the false one was twisted.

He worked his way back and forth along the slope, moving gradually upward. He was looking for a drip line. That was where little waterfalls and steady trickles of water poured down the slope during the winter rains. They carried the mycellium down and then mushrooms sprang up along the water's path.

In spite of being teased occasionally about being a bush boy, Jamie hadn't really been far off the road by himself. The forest was so thick that you could get lost just past the edge. The slope was covered in moss and ferns. There were the red rotting stumps of first-growth cedar that had been cut down many years before. Some of the oldest ones had rotted completely away and left large holes in the ground. Others were so soft that when he grabbed the wood, it came away like wet wool.

The chanterelles grew in the strangest places. Sometimes under logs. Other times under the moss itself. To find those, he had to watch for a hint of yellow showing through. Then he carefully pulled away the moss and eased out the mushroom. After that he didn't move again until he'd looked all around. He knew that where he found one, he'd find more. Seeing them was hard, though. When he first went with his father, he couldn't even see the ones that were under his feet.

The forest was so quiet it was spooky. Jamie could hear the rasp of his jacket. Overhead, the branches moved slightly, making a creaking sound. He was tempted to use a game trail rather than pull himself up the slope by holding onto bushes and trees. Climbing the game trails was much easier, but he didn't want to take a chance of meeting a cougar head on. There were lots of them around. Two had been spotted in people's yards in the last month. In July one had grabbed a kid staying at a nearby summer camp. The cougar had got him by the head and was trying to drag him away when the camp counselor bashed it on the head with a large stick.

After three hours, all he'd picked was about a kilogram of mushrooms. In a good year some people picked twenty or thirty kilos in a day. That's what he wanted. He wanted to go down to Joe's and have him weigh up the mushrooms and say, "That's a good day's picking."

He had to face up to it. There wasn't going to be any good picking until it rained. He bent back his head. Through the tops of the trees all he could see was blue sky.

When he got home his mom was sitting in the kitchen having a cup of coffee. She was staring out the window at the ocean. Usually when she did that, it meant something was wrong. He got himself a glass of milk and sat down with her.

"I got laid off," she said. "The mill's closing for two months. The price of lumber is down. Business is going to drop off. They're not waiting for it to happen."

The next day he kept looking at the sky, hoping for clouds. Usually in September it rained nearly every night. Instead, the sky was the same pale, whitish blue it was in summer. There wasn't a cloud to be seen.

A good rain was what he needed. The kind that started during the night and kept on for days until the forest floor was soaked and little waterfalls were tumbling over the cliffs.

He was leaning against his locker, hoping for rain, when Lance punched him in the arm. "Make a fortune, Mushroom King?"

Lance leaned close, glanced around to see if anyone was watching, then put his hand in his pocket and eased out a roll of bills. The outside bill was a fifty.

"You and me," Lance said, "we're friends. Twenty bucks for helping me out tomorrow."

"What about school?" Jamie said.

Lance shrugged. "Fine. I'll ask someone else. There's plenty of people want to make twenty bucks. Tell you what. I'll throw in an hour on my dirt bike. I wouldn't do that for anyone else."

"I don't know," Jamie said. Lance moved his lips but didn't make any sound. He didn't need to. Jamie knew exactly what he was saying. "Wimp."

The next morning Jamie started for school but, instead of going inside, he crossed over the soccer field and met Lance and Dopey and Grumpy among the trees at the back.

"What're we doing?" Jamie asked.

"Just going for a walk in the forest. Just like picking mushrooms."

"How're we going to make money that way?"

"Don't sweat it," Lance said. "You get twenty bucks no matter what. We do okay you get more. Maybe fifty. How often do you make fifty bucks? Here, guaranteed, ten bucks." He reached into his pocket and took out his roll of bills. He pulled out a ten and gave it to Jamie. "We're friends. Friends trust each other, right?"

They cut back through the trees to the edge of town. The three of them had their dirt bikes stashed in the bush. Jamie got on behind Lance. They led the way, racing over a logging road until they were in an area Jamie didn't know. They stopped and pushed the bikes off the road.

They hiked a game trail for half an hour.

The ground was steep. They crossed one ridge, went down the far side, then up another ridge. Jamie felt in his pocket. He'd brought his father's compass with him. It was easy to lose your way in a place like this. Once you lost it, it was hard to get your sense of direction back. Moss grew everywhere, not just on the north side of the trees. The trees blocked out the sun. Even on the top of a ridge the forest was so thick and the ridges so uneven that you couldn't see the ocean.

"That's cougar scat," Jamie said. He bent down to inspect it. "It's fresh."

"You're always worrying about something, Bush Boy. You think a cougar's suddenly going to appear and chomp on us? We've been here lots of times. Never seen a cougar. Never seen a bear. Never seen no dragons."

"Never seen no cops, either," Grumpy said.

"No helicopters," Dopey added.

They started laughing but Lance waved his hand for them to be quiet. He pointed to one side of a blowdown. They were at the top of a ridge and looking down the slope.

The blowdown was the biggest Jamie had ever seen. There had to have been a twister.

Trees were uprooted or snapped off and piled on each other at every angle.

Jamie hoped they weren't going into the blowdown. They were very dangerous. He'd been going to look for mushrooms in one once and his father had called him back. When he'd wanted to know why, his father had said, "Let's just stop for a break and watch." As they rested, they heard a sudden creaking, and one of the trees slipped under the pressure and sprang loose.

Lance led them to the blowdown, then along its edge. Dopey had been carrying a pack sack. Lance took it and handed it to Jamie. He motioned for Jamie to follow. Dopey and Grumpy brought up the rear. Lance crept forward until they came to an area that was more open.

"Now you earn your money, Bush Boy."

"What do I do?"

"There's a plantation there. Lots of lovely plants just ready to be harvested. You pick the leaves and put them in the sack. When it's full, you come back. You get a full sack, you get your fifty."

Jamie didn't move.

"What's the matter, Bush Boy? Scared?"

Jamie was scared. Everyone knew there were marijuana plantations around. People were always joking about it. But the mushroom pickers, if they stumbled on one, left right away. The growers used government land because that way if the Mounties found the plot, no one could be charged. The trouble was, anyone could come and pick the plants. There were stories of long-haired types sleeping right in the middle of their crops when they were ready for picking. They carried machetes and guns.

"You gonna buy a dirt bike picking bottles? You want something, you gotta take some risks. You fill the pack and you get a bonus. A hundred bucks total."

A hundred dollars, Jamie thought. There was a sign up at the grocery store advertising a second-hand bike for $185.

He grabbed the pack sack and crawled forward. Then he stopped.

Some things, he thought, weren't worth doing. That's what his dad had said when they were out picking and they saw a doe. Jamie had told his dad to shoot it, but his dad said there were some things that weren't worth doing. He'd brought a gun because there were cougars in the area, not to shoot a deer out of season.

Jamie was just starting to crawl backward when he heard someone yell. Behind him he heard Lance say, "Get out of here."

Jamie glanced back. He just caught a glimpse of Lance and Dopey and Grumpy as they fled. He stood up.

The grower had been looking at the other three. Now he saw Jamie and turned. He was carrying a machete. He swore and charged. There was a large fallen-down tree behind Jamie. He dropped to his knees and scrambled under. The grower had to climb over the tree. It slowed him down and gave Jamie a bit of a lead.

Jamie couldn't think. He ran into a tree, got knocked sideways, stumbled and kept running. There was no way that he could outrun his pursuer.

The blowdown was directly ahead of him. He plunged into it. He scrambled onto a large tree and ran along the trunk, grabbing at the branches to stay upright. Behind him he could hear the grower swearing and yelling. There was no time to plan anything. He had to keep jumping from tree to tree.

All at once the tree he was on moved and, with a yell, he fell sideways. He thrashed through the branches. When he hit the ground, he scrambled forward on his hands and knees until he hit his head against a root. He lay there, his heart pounding. All around him the branches crisscrossed. Here and there openings appeared.

He tried to control his breathing. His chest ached from running. He could hear the grower walking along the trunks. The blowdown was like a maze. There was no way of knowing which direction was which in the tangle of branches and trunks.

Jamie was just starting to crawl away when overhead he heard a boot scuff on a log. He looked up.

The grower was standing directly above him. He swung the machete and chopped off a branch. It looked like he was going to climb down into the tangle.

Just then there was a crack. Jamie knew the sound of a tree pulling loose. The grower paused.

"I know you're there somewhere," the man yelled. "If I catch you, you're dead meat. You've been picking my crop for the last couple of weeks. You come back and you're dead. You hear me? You're dead."

With that he disappeared. Jamie didn't move. He wasn't going to be tricked. In a few minutes, he heard the boots scuff wood close by. He'd been right. The grower had been pretending to leave. Now he really left, his departure marked with curses and threats that gradually faded.

Jamie didn't dare climb back onto the logs. At least here he was safe for the moment. If he had to he could stay until it was dark. Then he could creep out of the blowdown by the light of the moon.

Suddenly he remembered the cougar spoor. Jamie looked around. The branches seemed to form an endless series of caves filled with shadows. In amongst the branches he wouldn't have a chance if a cougar was prowling. Staying where he was didn't seem like such a good idea.

Then he remembered his father's compass. He would have to go around and through the trees, but it would keep him going in the right direction.

He took it out. It wasn't broken. It had a strong metal case and it would take more than a tumble off a tree to break it.

He wormed his way through the branches. Sometimes he had to crawl on his stomach. Sometimes he crawled on his knees. Sometimes he was able to stand upright. Finally, he was peering from the edge of the blowdown. He looked around, then slipped into the forest.

When he got back to the road, the three bikes were gone. Lance hadn't even waited to see if he was okay.

Jamie didn't get home until supper time. The school had called to see why he wasn't in class. He told his parents he'd gone dirt-bike riding with Lance. He was grounded for a week and his mother gave him a lecture on all the times he'd got in trouble with Lance in the past.

"There are times..." she said. Since he wasn't going anywhere except school for a week, his father handed him an ax and suggested he work his way through the woodpile.

On Monday he saw Lance and Dopey and

Grumpy huddled at one end of the hall.

"How are you, Bush Boy," Lance said. "We looked for you but you didn't keep up. You've got to learn to move faster."

"He said you've been picking his crop for weeks. You knew he would be watching,"

"No hard feelings," Lance said. "Sometimes things happen. Here. For your trouble."

He held out a ten-dollar bill. Jamie looked at it, then at Dopey and Grumpy. They were both grinning.

He'd had some good times with Lance— jumping off roofs, climbing over the fence into the salvage yard to see what they could find, riding their bikes off the end of the dock. Every time he'd held back, Lance would charge ahead, yelling, "Wimp. Wimp."

If the two stooges hadn't been there, Jamie might have asked what had happened. Lance probably would just have smiled with the left side of his mouth and shrugged his shoulders. They'd both have known the question wasn't just about Lance running and leaving Jamie alone.

"I don't want it," Jamie said. He took the ten Lance had already given him and held it out. When Lance didn't take it, Jamie let the bill drop to the floor.

They stood there staring at each other. Lance looked to the side.

"Ah, what do I care. Come on, you guys," he said to Dopey and Grumpy. "You make your choices, Bush Boy." He turned away and retreated down the hall, becoming smaller and smaller until he and his pals turned the corner and disappeared.

The Divorced Kids Club

Mr. Turner wore T-shirts and running shoes with everything, including his blue suit. I heard him telling my mom that he had fifty-six sweatshirts. He had his first team sweatshirt framed. It hung on his office wall.

He had two kids. Jimmy was a year older than me. Billy was a year younger. That put me in the middle. When you're in the middle, you're not the oldest and you're not the baby. You're nobody. If he and my mom became an item, I was going to go from being queen of the castle to being a nobody, with no time to adjust.

From the moment my father moved out, my mother started saying, "It's not your fault, Kathleen." She'd read in some magazine that kids blame themselves for their parents' breakups, and she was always checking to make sure that I wasn't weighed down with guilt. But I was way ahead of her on the topic of kids and divorce. There were seven kids in my class with separated or divorced parents, and we formed this sort of club. There were all the official school clubs—the Drama Club and the Library Club—but the Divorced Kids Club was unofficial. My folks were only separated so I wasn't a full member, only an associate. We never had any set times for meetings and nobody was president. We sort of hung together—sometimes more, sometimes less, depending on what was happening. We'd hear that someone's parents had split up and we let them know that it'd be okay if they joined us beside the front steps in good weather or in the library in bad.

We weren't super organized, but sometimes one of us would read an article about kids and family in the paper, then report on it. The articles were always by adults. A lot of it was off base but now and again there'd be something worth knowing. If nothing else it told us how adults thought. A couple of us had seen shrinks. After a session we rehashed the shrink stuff and sorted out the wheat from the chaff. Most of it was chaff.

It's not like we were a therapy group or anything. It's just that sometimes it helped to get advice from someone who'd been through it. Joey was our expert. His mom had been divorced three times. He knew the moves better than anyone. Marilyn's dad was always falling in love. Every couple of months he got goofy. Marilyn quit learning his girlfriends' names after number seven. She gave me a list of the signs.

Compared to some of the others, I was lucky. My mom had a job, so after my dad left, we weren't worrying about having to sleep in some shelter. "We're going to have to adjust," she said to me, but our lives mostly stayed the same. Some of the kids in the Group had lots of adjusting to do. Their dad leaves, they have to move out of the house, into a new neighborhood, new school, make new friends. We stayed in our apartment. It's just that Dad wasn't at the breakfast table anymore or making peanut brittle or fudge in the evenings. On weekends he'd pick me up after school and then he'd bring me back on Sunday at noon.

Some of the other kids had parents who were fighting the Hundred Year War. Not mine.

While I got my stuff ready for the weekend, they'd stand in the doorway and catch up on news. Sometimes my dad would even have tea. It was just that he sort of sat on the edge of the chair instead of leaning back. I kept hoping that my mom would ask him to stay for supper but I knew it was hopeless. Most people have day-books divided into fifteen-minute sections. His was divided into five-minute sections and there weren't any blank spaces. He even had spaces marked Relaxation. He used Hi-liters to color-code his activities: green for work, red for non-work events, orange for meetings. I was red.

"Why can't you guys just get back together?" I asked my mom one Sunday evening. She just stroked my hair. I wasn't really expecting an explanation. Dad's the explainer.

My mom lives on her emotions. She feels an emotion and she's off following it. One year it was the thrill of white-water rafting. Another time it was the mystery of hiking in the Himalayas. I don't remember the Himalayas because I was only two. My dad says she's a spontaneous enthusiast. Most of her enthusiasms, if she gets to do them, last two to three months.

My dad tries to keep us all safe. He does all the prep work, checks on accommodation, sees what the reputation of the company is like that's offering the adventure, talks to a few people who've already done whatever it is that she wants to do. This year she wanted to buy a boat and sail to Australia. She figured it would take us eleven months. My dad said fine but first we'd have to take sailing lessons and navigation courses. He was hoping, I think, that before the courses were over, she'd be back to her watercolor painting.

Jimmy and Billy were wannabe jocks. They were into soccer and weight lifting and lacrosse. Since Mr. Turner started coming around, we'd been sitting on a lot of bleachers.

I didn't understand my mom. Even with Dad living in an apartment on the other side of town, everything was going along fine. It wasn't like we needed Mr. Turner to rescue us. Mom and I were a pretty good team. We shared the chores and after supper if she didn't have to work, we'd microwave some popcorn and watch a movie. Both my folks still came to watch me figure skate. They just sat with a foot of space between them. I've been figure skating since I was five. My dad says that when I was five, I called it hockey twirling.

I wanted just the two of us—or even better, the three of us—to go to our cabin for the weekend. It's built on the old homestead. My mom's family has lived on the property since 1876.

Mom looked sort of guilty when she told me she'd asked Mr. Turner and the two little Turners to share our weekend. I guess I shouldn't have been surprised. The Group said it would happen. It's like your world is solid and then there's this earthquake. You start to rebuild and then there's a trembler, and everything gets knocked over again.

It's not that there was anything wrong with Mr. Turner, other than the fact that he was Mr. Turner. He didn't get drunk or scream or yell. He washed regularly.

He was one of our gym teachers. That's how he and Mom met. She was at the school for a parents' night. They bumped into each other in the hallway and started talking. If I had known they'd meet and start talking, I wouldn't have brought the notice home. That's the trouble with life. You do something and you have no idea how it's going to turn out.

"Aren't Jimmy and Billy nice?" my mom whispered to me after we arrived at the cabin.

"Not particularly," I said. You don't want direct answers, you shouldn't ask direct questions. They were always grunting and sweating. They weren't into reading unless it was manuals on how to take some machine apart. Some people are anti-abortion, some are anti-war, some are anti-whaling. They were anti-muffler.

"Be nice," my mother said. She's into nice in a big way. It's the only complaint I've got about her. That and the way she does her hair.

My father plays the cello. If you know anything about cellos, that's all you need to know.

My mom used to play the violin. She played in the symphony. That's how they met. She must have been pretty good because she was first violin. She quit after I was born and by the time she could leave me with a babysitter she was more interested in getting a job that paid decent money. Even two people playing in the symphony doesn't pay for having adventures.

The best times were when we'd go out to the cabin and my dad would practice his music and my mom would paint and I'd read.

Sometimes, my mom would get out her violin and they'd play together. I liked that a lot. In December, we'd always come out for the holiday and once in awhile there'd be glare ice so I could practice my figure skating. If you've never seen glare ice, you're missing something. It forms when the weather turns suddenly cold and there's no wind. It's like a mirror as far as you can see in any direction. Not a bump. Not a mark. Do you know what it's like to go down to the beach, build a fire, then sit, lacing up your skates? I'd stand there for minutes looking at the ice before I'd finally push off, leaving these curving lines behind me. My folks always let me make the first marks on the ice.

When we got to the cabin we discovered there wasn't much dry wood. My dad was the one who always took care of the details. With him gone nobody had ordered firewood. We had to dig out wood left outside from the year before, then knock the pieces apart because the frost had welded them together. Lucky there were some sticks in the wood box. That got us started. My mom and I stood some of the frozen wood on end on top of the heater. You could hear the drips sizzling as they hit the hot metal.

There was nothing at the cottage to dismantle. No old car motors or motorcycles needing to be fixed. No weights to lift. I thought the trolls were going to have nervous breakdowns. They kept sitting down, then getting up, then pacing around the room, then going outside, then coming in, then sitting down. They must have done that a hundred times. Once we'd got the cabin warm, my mom should have been taking out her paints and I should have been wrapping myself in my old quilt with the seven dwarfs on it and reading one of my books. Instead, there was all this clumping and clomping around the room.

The trolls wanted to go hunting. They hadn't brought snowshoes and the drifts must have been higher than my waist. It probably was what they needed. An hour of wading through deep snow and they'd have been down for the night.

I was wondering who was going to sleep where. There were only two bedrooms—my folks' and mine. I hoped my mom and Mr. Turner weren't going to sleep in my folks' room. Some of the Group said they didn't care about that but I didn't believe it. It wasn't like our folks shouldn't date or anything, but they could leave the other stuff until after we'd left home. Or do it where we didn't have to deal with it.

I didn't need to worry. My mom and I slept in one room and Mr. Turner and the trolls slept in the other.

Before we went to sleep, my mom gave me a hug and said, "Your dad and I aren't getting back together. We're just not compatible."

"I want him playing his cello again," I said. I felt like when I was figure skating and about to try some new move and didn't know how it would work out. "I want to go and tell him when it's time to have tea and raisin bread."

She lay on her back and I could tell her eyes were open even in the dark. "I don't know how it happened," she said. When she said that, I thought about my cousin. He's just around one year old and when you put something under a blanket, he doesn't know it's there. It's just gone. I know that when he's older, he'll know it hasn't stopped existing. He'll dig around and pull it from under the blanket. It makes me wonder about my mom.

In the morning, they made bacon and eggs

and hash browns, but I stuck to cheese and bread and a pear. I'm not a vegetarian or anything but I like quiet food. I don't mean I'm against celery. I like celery. It's not that kind of noisy that I mean. Peaceful food maybe is what I mean. There's unpeaceful food like roast beast killed with spears, skinned and cooked over a spit. People cut off bloody hunks and rip it apart with their teeth. Asparagus is peaceful. Avocados filled with shrimp. Honey on fresh-baked bread. Pancakes with bananas and syrup. Nobody snarls and grunts when they're eating Brie.

The trolls were hunched over waiting to go out and kill something. Mr. Turner had brought a .22 so they could have some target practice. When they opened the door, a drift higher than their heads greeted them. Mr. Turner's Bronco was buried.

The last time the snow drifted like this, the folks and I just hunkered down for a week and spent Christmas at the cabin with a little tree that we'd decorated with popcorn. What I remember most is that some sparrows were so tired and weak that we had to pick them up and bring them inside. We put them in a cardboard box and fed them water and sunflower seeds.

Turner & Sons trudged out to the road. They came back in a few minutes. "There's been no traffic. No sign of tracks," he said. I could have told him that. When there's a wind, the snow piles into shoulder-high drifts on the curves. The longer it blows, the harder the snow. Two days of wind and you can walk on top of the drifts and not break through.

My mom said, "We have to have more wood." She wasn't in a panic or anything, but I'd seen her checking how much wood was in the box. We were good until noon probably.

We all went out to dig around in the snow. We found some bits of old lumber and a few pieces of punky birch. They wouldn't throw much heat but it was better than nothing.

"We can burn the furniture," Jimmy said. "I seen that once in the movies. They were on a steamboat and they broke up the furniture." He sounded like he wanted to get at it right away.

"Not a lot of BTU's in furniture," I said. I didn't care if they froze to death; they weren't getting my books and bookshelf.

Mr. Turner rummaged around in the shack behind the cabin and came up with my dad's ax and saw. The three of them went off to cut some stove wood. He's like my mom in that he believes in being spontaneous. He's always talking about how much fun it is to have pick-up games. His classes are a bit like that. You're never quite sure what you might be doing next. He'll have an idea, then he gets a better idea.

"I hope," I said, "he knows to cut up a dead tree." He might be a jock but he was a city jock. Cutting a green tree would have been a waste of time. The wood is too wet to burn.

"He's got a degree," my mother replied. "It's hanging in his office."

When we were back in the cabin, I said, "Do you think Dad brings anybody up here?" I was thinking about long-haired Jennifer. She played the viola. She was in the symphony and in a quintet with my dad. She was always asking my dad questions when it was obvious she already knew the answers. After a recital I heard her telling him what great hands he had and how inspiring he was for her. She'd only been out of music school for a few years.

"I don't think so," my mother said, with that pause in her voice that meant she'd just had an unexpected thought. Dad was somebody who was always predictable. Once when the Group did visualization exercises, I visualized him as Clark Kent. I visualized Mr. Turner as a wannabe Superman. Biggest, fastest, highest, longest, heaviest were important words to him. At school he spent his time careening around the gym. After hours he was always playing basketball or floor hockey and yelling. With him in the game, you didn't need an audience to make noise.

When I raised the question of how my mother could go from silence and Argyles to noise and sweat socks, the Group said, "Sometimes a change is as good as a rest."

That was when Billy charged through the door. He was blubbering and yelling and waving his arms so much we couldn't make any sense out of what he was saying. When Mom got him calmed down, we pulled on our parkas and followed him. There was this trail in the snow. It led to a forty-foot spruce tree. It had been the biggest tree on our property.

My mother had just started to say,

"Where's…" when Jimmy's head suddenly appeared among the branches.

"He's here," he screamed.

We thrashed through the snow. Mr. Turner was lying on his back under the tree. Given the size of the tree, I thought he must be dead. I'd never seen a dead person and I didn't want to see one now so I concentrated on his boots. One was pointed straight up but the other went off at a weird angle.

"Mike?" my mother said. Her voice had that high, quavery sound it gets when she's scared.

"I think my leg's broken," he said.

The branches were huge. It was lucky one of them hadn't gone right through him. "Where's the ax?" Billy asked.

"I had it in my hand," Mr. Turner said.

Jimmy rummaged around in the snow, then held it up. He was going to start whacking away at the tree but my mother stopped him. She told him we didn't want to do anything that would make the tree move. Those green branches were like giant springs.

The saw was back at the stump. We took turns sawing off the branches close to him. The tree trunk went right across his stomach. He should have been mushed. The snow had saved his life.

"Maybe," my mother said, "we can dig him out. Go get the shovel."

We dug until we saw the grass at his head and feet. Then we dug along both sides. We slid the shovel underneath him and pulled out the snow.

When he was loose, we all dragged him out by his shoulders. Every so often the tree would give a twitch. My mother would hold up her hand. We'd freeze in place.

We loaded him onto the toboggan and towed him back to the cabin. His leg had a kink in it halfway between the ankle and the knee, and there was a piece of bone sticking out. For the first time since I'd met them, Jimmy and Billy were quiet.

I looked at the lake. This year there'd been a wind so the ice was rough and in places it was pebbly. I could see patches of snow but the wind had blown the ice mostly clear. "I'll bet the Bjornsons are down. Maybe they'll have a cellular."

"You can't," my mother said. "We've got to

stay here until the snow plow comes through."

I looked at Mr. Turner. His face looked like gray playdough. If the bullets he'd brought had been bigger, I'd have given him one to bite on. Here we were, going for a weekend of fun and games, real casual like, and suddenly everything was serious.

"We'll hike out on the road," Jimmy said.

"You won't get far in the snow," my mom said. "You'll die standing up."

"I'll go," I said. I went and got my skates. "On the lake. I can skate faster than anyone can run."

"You can't," Mom said. "I won't let you."

I looked at her, I looked at the pathetic little pile of wood, I looked at Mr. Turner. Band-Aids and a few painkillers weren't going to do it for him. I put on my parka and wrapped a wool scarf around my face. My mom went down to the lake with me.

"I'm sorry," she said. She was looking at the sky. The clouds went right to the horizon. "If it starts snowing, you turn back. If you get to the Bjornsons and nobody is there, you turn back. You stay close to the shore."

I slung my boots around my neck and started. It's easy to be brave when you can still see back to where you've begun. At the first point of land the ice was bad and I had to go out until I started to worry about losing sight of the shore. The ice around the reef is in layers. There's been ice, then the ice has flooded and made a second, thin skin. You step on this skin and you suddenly drop down. It's a good way to break an ankle.

It was so still I could hear my skates on the ice and the sound of my nylon jacket rubbing as I swung my arms. I figured it was half an hour to the Bjornsons' place. I was sure I saw smoke coming from their chimney when we went past the day before.

Skating kept me warm. The ice was pretty good. There were places where it was pebbled and I had to be careful not to trip, and some places close to shore the ice was dirty, with bits of grass and mud, even small stones. I went far-ther out to avoid these, but I kept the dark line of the shore constantly in sight. I was grateful that there wasn't much glare. Even a little while on the ice on a bright day and people go snow blind. My dad made us snow glasses out of cardboard and string. We used them when we ice fished. They kept out too much light that makes your eyes feel like they're full of sand.

"Safely," he was always saying. "Do what you're going to do but do it safely." He was always checking and double-checking.

I wasn't breathing too hard by the time I reached the Bjornsons. I didn't see any smoke from their chimney but I changed into my boots and waded through the snow.

There were no fresh footprints. I didn't bother going right up to the cabin. The drifted snow didn't have a mark on it. I trudged back to the lake and put on my skates. My mother had said to turn back but there were more cabins not too much farther on. I figured there had to be someone in one of them.

To get to them, I had to round another point. That meant skating a fair ways out, then back into the bay. There were no buildings on this bay. At the next point I noticed a skim of snow cutting over the ice. Just thin lines of it. I didn't like that.

I thought about Rhonda then. She was part of the Group. Her dad had tattoos. Not eeny-weeny ones, like a heart on his bicep that said Mom, but all over. He had snakes and skulls and flowers crawling up his arms. She said when he took off his shirt, he was a real picture show. When she asked her mom how come she'd married him, her mom said, "I couldn't think of anything that would upset my folks more." That gave us all something to think about. When you're little you think the giants know everything. Then you get older and the world gets real scary because you realize they may be bigger but they aren't always using a compass that works.

By the time I reached the first cabin there were a few snowflakes. They landed on my jacket and disappeared. I skated in closer to shore. No smoke from the chimney. There was no one at the second or third cabin, either.

I wished I'd thought ahead and towed the toboggan. I could have loaded it with wood and towed it back. I wished my dad was with us. He'd have insisted we sit down and discuss alternatives. We could have put Mr. Turner on the toboggan and towed him to the Bjornsons' cabin. There was a woodpile there. We could have broken a window to get in. They wouldn't mind as long as we replaced the glass. We could have waited for help there.

The wind was coming from the east. The skiffs of snow were turning into streamers and the flakes were steadier. This wasn't, I realized, a good situation.

I shouldn't have left without matches and a candle. I'd been too spontaneous the last few months. I'd got too used to getting an idea and jumping up and doing it without stopping to think about it first. If I was unable to go forward or back and had to find shelter, matches would let me start a fire and warm up a cabin or, if worse came to worst, to keep warm in a snow cave.

At least I'd brought a small thermos of tea and my boots. If I had to walk, they'd keep my feet warm. My mom had pushed a couple of oatmeal cookies into my pocket. I stopped and ate one. There was no smoke and no lights anywhere along the shore.

The next bay was filled with reefs and rock. I had to go farther out. That made me nervous. If the snow really started, I'd lose sight of the shoreline. The wind was still blowing shoreward but I knew how quickly it could turn.

Ever since I was little I'd heard about one of the first settlers. He and a friend started walking from Gimli to Hecla Island. In those days it wasn't called Hecla. It was called Mikley, which means Big Island. They were pulling a sleigh loaded with supplies. Flour, pemmican, beans, sugar, salt. The weather was clear. Nice bright blue sky. Then it clouded over and a wind sprang up. They lost sight of the shore but they weren't concerned. They knew the direction of the wind. But at some time the wind changed and they didn't realize it. They walked all day and most of the night. They would have died, but my great-great-uncle had put a lantern in his window just in case someone was out there in the storm. They stumbled in. One of them lost a couple of toes but the other had to have both his feet amputated. After his legs healed, he went around on his knees clearing his land.

Whenever I wanted to try something new that my dad thought was dangerous, he would say, "Make sure you know which direction the wind is blowing."

My mom and Mr. Turner had decided on the spur of the moment to go to the cabin. They were on the phone and Mr. Turner was saying to my mom how he loved tobogganing when he was a boy and kids never got a chance to go tobogganing nowadays and she said, "Let's do it." We were on the road in an hour, the two of them in the front and me and trolls in the back. The trolls were nearly gibbering because they were going to conquer the wilderness. The weather was absolutely clear and bright. Everything was nice and sparkly.

I finished my cookie and was glad to get my hand back inside my mitten. I had gloves on, but outside my mitten they didn't keep my fingers warm. I started skating again.

If this was Russia, I thought, wolves would be chasing me. There were wolves around but they were pretty shy. When we went out with some of the fishermen to watch them lift nets, my father got some good pictures of wolves. They followed the fishermen to eat the garbage fish that were left on the ice.

I crossed the next point and ran smack into a pressure ridge. I skated close to it. It was made of huge slabs of ice that had got pushed up into a line twice as tall as I was. There was no climbing over it. I skated along it until I was way out, then walked over the rough ice where the ridge disappeared.

I knew I was too far from shore. I should have gone back, I was thinking. When I got to the Bjornsons, I should have gone back to our cabin and got them all and we could have trekked over the ice. I figured this was how people got in trouble—not all at once but a little at a time.

The wind was blowing harder so there was a steady ankle-high drift. I looked at the horizon and realized the light was starting to fade. That's when I got scared. When it's cloudy, it gets dark really early and there wasn't going to be any moon.

I felt like there was something or someone behind me. I turned around but no one was there. My breathing sounded really loud. Dumb, dumb, dumb, I kept saying to myself. What direction was the wind?

I had to bend over and squeeze my thighs to get my legs to quit shaking. I drank the last of the tea, then started skating. It was harder to see what the ice was like.

I hit something and my feet went out from underneath me. I sprawled forward. I skidded in a half circle before I managed to stop. I hadn't hurt myself but when I stood up, I realized that one mitten was gone. I looked for it but the wind must have carried it toward the shore. The chance of finding a white mitten on white snow in the gathering dark wasn't very big. I pulled my hand inside my sleeve.

I'm going to die, I thought. My stupid parents can't get along and I'm going to die. That's when I got angry. I thought about the Group. We'd thrashed this one around lots of times. Someone, probably Joey, said kids were collateral damage. Killed by friendly fire. He was into war in a big way. He knew all about Vietnam and terrorists and Desert Storm. Schwarzkopf was his hero. Last Halloween when we were all having a bad time, he got us to put on army uniforms and bandages and casts. We went to the school party as the walking wounded. We had ketchup everywhere. When we went out for treats, dogs kept running up and licking it off.

I started to cry. Then I stopped because the tears were freezing on my cheeks. I yelled for help and then I pulled my scarf off my face and whistled as loudly as I could.

That's when a dog barked. I stood there listening. I was floating in space. There was the darkness and there was me and there was the barking. I couldn't go fast anymore because I was afraid of falling again. It was like skating inside this big black room.

Then I saw a light. I stopped and stared. I wasn't even sure that it was real. I waited for it to disappear. When it didn't, I started to skate toward it. It was a pinpoint of light. I didn't dare take my eyes off it.

When I finally got close, it went off. I said, "No," out loud. Just like that. I kept staring into the darkness waiting for it to go back on. When it didn't, I kept my eyes focused on the spot where I last saw it. The shore was just this dark line. I couldn't even tell if there was a gap in the trees.

I picked my way along the shore until I came to a snowmobile path. I didn't even try to take off my skates. I kept whistling and the dog kept barking as I clumped along the path. The first thing I saw was a fish shed, then a low building. A husky was chained up beside a shelter made from a couple of boxes and canvas.

I banged on the door. There was a truck parked and I figured there had to be somebody home so I banged on the door some more.

At last a light went on. Then someone called, "Who's there?"

"Me. There's been an accident. We need help."

The door opened and there was this old guy in his longjohns. He switched on a flashlight. Before he could ask who I was, his wife turned on the porch light. She was wearing this long blue housecoat and had her head tied in a scarf.

"For heaven's sakes, Henry!" she said. "Get her in here."

Henry dragged me inside. He pushed me into a chair while Maude undid my scarf. It was covered in large ice balls made by my breath.

Then she undid my parka and pulled it off. "I'll make tea," she said. Henry went to unlace my skates.

"Don't touch them," I yelled. It was like they were huge. "I don't want to lose my feet."

"You've frozen your toes," he said, "but I don't think you'll lose your feet. The feeling will come back in a few minutes. Then we can get your skates off. Why in heaven's name were you out figure skating at night?"

"I wasn't figure skating," I said between

yelling and groaning as my feet thawed.

Henry brought a basin of cool water. When the pain had stopped enough, he undid my laces and pulled off my skates. "Here, put your feet in this. Never mind your socks."

I explained who I was, about the accident and no wood. Maude gave me tea. I gulped it down and she refilled my cup. Henry had disappeared. He came back fully dressed.

"Damn fools," he said. "I'm going to Larry's. He can go to town for a doctor. Then I'll take a sled of wood."

After awhile my feet felt like they were back to their regular size. Maude peeled off my socks and dried my feet. "Are they going to have to be amputated?" I asked.

She shook her head. "You might lose your toenails. That happened to me once. It's okay, they grow back."

She helped me get undressed, wrapped me in three blankets, propped me up on the couch, then fed me the leftovers from their supper of stew and mashed potatoes. I ate three large slices of bread with butter and honey and drank an entire pot of tea with canned milk and sugar.

We sat there talking until I fell asleep. I told Maude how scared I had been that I'd have to have my feet cut off. She knew all about the guy who'd got amputated. He was Henry's grandfather. She'd been friends with my grandmother when they were girls. "We're all connected every which way," she said. "We just lose track of each other sometimes with all this coming and going that people do nowadays."

They drove a doctor to our place on a snowmobile. He took care of Mr. Turner. They couldn't use a helicopter because of the low clouds, so one of the fishermen took him to the nearest hospital in a Bombardier.

Maude and I got to talk lots. She and Henry had been married fifty years. She said he wasn't perfect by a long shot but then neither was she. "I wanted Errol Flynn," she said, "but he was busy so I took Henry." She figured they'd managed by making compromises. "Nobody always gets the head, nobody always gets the tail," she said. I asked her if she had a formula, one that maybe others could use. She said when she and Henry were having a fight one time because they were not compatible about something, she decided to make sweet and sour spareribs. "I was looking and looking for an answer and there it was right in front of me in that old cookbook of mine. If you put in sugar and sugar, it's too sweet. If you put in vinegar and vinegar, it's too sour."

Once the road was open, my mom came with Mr. Turner's Bronco. When I was leaving, Maude gave me half a dozen butter tarts. She asked me to come back and visit her the next time we came out. I sat up front with my mom. I told her about all the stuff Maude and I had talked about.

Billy and Jimmy sat in the back.

There are some things too serious to talk about. That's what Rhonda says. Something happens and from then on that thing affects everything you do for the rest of your life. It's always there, sort of like the cornerstone in a building.

When we got back to the city after taking Jimmy and Billy to their aunt's place, then checking on Mr. Turner in the hospital, my mom and I didn't have much to say to each other. I knew she felt guilty and that was fine with me. I didn't like the fact that Henry and Maude thought I was one of those damn fools.

I was glad she didn't keep saying she was sorry because that would just have meant she figured it was over and everything was okay.

My dad came to see that I was all right. I showed him my toenails. The ones on my big toes were turning black. Maude said once they died right back, I'd be able to lift them off.

My mom did say to me that she thought I was incredibly brave, not just because I went for help but because I went for help for someone I didn't particularly like. I didn't tell her that the reason I was determined to get help was because I know my mom. If Mr. Turner had been crippled, she'd have blamed herself and, even if she didn't love him, she'd have felt obliged to take care of him. If he'd died, she'd have spontaneously offered to take in the trolls. There are some fates worse than death.

◆

My dad stayed for tea one evening. After we had tea, my mom noticed that he didn't have his daybook with him. She asked him if he'd like to stay for supper. When he came back the next evening, he stayed to watch TV and since it was so late, he slept on the couch. In a week or so, he moved back into their bedroom. They must have sorted some things out because he quit turning a trip to the store into a safari to darkest Africa, and Mom quit looking unhappy if she couldn't dash out of the house without waiting to turn off the burners on the stove.

I'm out of the club now but I stay in touch. Rhonda's trying to set up a twelve-step program. Joey's talking about applying for a government grant. He's glad for me but he wishes I were still a part of the Group. He wants me to help him incorporate and franchise Divorced Kids Clubs in schools all across North America. He says he's going to become a divorce lawyer who specializes in the interests of kids.

This spring when my dad and my mom and me went up to the cabin, we stopped and gave Henry and Maude the biggest box of chocolates we'd been able to find.

Henry said, "How's the leg? Holding up okay?"

"Yeah, fine," Dad said. "Fit as a fiddle." He didn't want to embarrass anyone by saying it wasn't him who'd dropped a tree on himself.

On this trip, I had my bag of books. Dad

had his cello. Mom had her watercolors. She brought her violin with her. We brought two boxes of popcorn and enough sugar to make peanut brittle for an army.

"Thank goodness you had your light on that night," my father said to Henry.

"What light?" Henry asked.

"That light I saw in your window," I said.

"No light," Maude replied. She was serving my father one of her butter tarts. "We went to bed early that night. We were planning on getting up at four o'clock to start for town on the snowmobile. Must have been some moonlight reflecting on the window."

My folks both looked at me kind of funny. I'd told them about the light and how I followed it to shore.

Pulling out of their driveway, my dad said, "They probably left the light on, then one of them turned it off without remembering. We all do that sometimes. It's one of those little things you do automatically. I went out for the newspaper the other day, checked on the mail as I went by, then when I went in, I didn't remember that the mailbox had been empty."

"Sounds good to me," I said. I wasn't going

to argue with him. I know for sure there wasn't any moon that night. Old people are forgetful. That's a fact. I can deal with that.